Women of Influence

Women of Influence

Bonnie Burnard

Coteau Books

Some of the stories in this collection have appeared as follows: "Nice Girls Don't Tell" adapted for broadcast as a radio drama aired on CBC's "Morningside"; "Music Lessons" in *NeWest Review* and adapted for broadcast as a TV drama aired on CBC; "The Replacement," formerly titled "Windows" appeared in *Coming Attractions* (Oberon, 1983), broadcast on CBC Radio's "Ambience" and adapted for broadcast as a radio drama aired on CBC's "Morningside"; "Grizzly Mountain" appeared in *Coming Attractions* (Oberon, 1983); "Joyride" appeared in *Dinosaur Review*; "Women of Influence" was aired on CBC Radio's "Ambience"; "The Appointment" appeared in *NeWest Review*; "The Knife Sharpener" adapted for broadcast as a radio drama on CBC's "Morningside"; "Moon Watcher" was published in *Best Canadian Stories* (Oberon, 1984) and in *More Saskatchewan Gold* (Coteau, 1984); "Wolf Spiders" was published in *Prism International*; "Landscape" was aired on CBC Radio's "Ambience" and adapted for broadcast as a radio drama aired on CBC's "Morningside"; and "Reflections" appeared in *Coming Attractions* (Oberon, 1983), in *Saskatchewan Gold* (Coteau, 1982) and adapted for broadcast as a radio drama aired on CBC's "Morningside."

Cover painting: "The Pooka and the Rat-Catcher's Wife" by Elyse Yates St. George. Reproduced on *Women of Influence* courtesy of the artist.
Cover and book design by Coteau Books.
Typeset by Type Systems, Regina.
Printed by Hignell Printing, Winnipeg.

The author would like to thank the Saskatchewan Arts Board and the City of Regina for their financial assistance, Edna Alford for her editorial counsel, and the members of the Bombay Bicycle Club for their generous and constant support.

The publisher gratefully acknowledges the financial assistance of the Saskatchewan Arts Board, the Canada Council, the Department of Communications and the City of Regina.

Canadian Cataloguing in Publication Data
Burnard, Bonnie, 1945-
   Women of influence
   (McCourt fiction series; 5)

   ISBN 0-919926-81-9 (bound) — ISBN 0-919926-82-7 (pbk.)

I. Title. II. Series.

PS8553.V75W6 1988 C813'.54 C88-098105-9
PR9199.3.B87W6 1988

with the assistance of the
Saskatchewan
Arts Board

COTEAU BOOKS
Suite 401 – 2206 Dewdney Avenue
Regina, Saskatchewan
Canada S4R 1H3

Contents

for D'Arcy, Melanie and David,
and for D.

Nice Girls Don't Tell

"He had the hairiest back," Dutch says. "Like an ape."

She stands behind the couch with her hip cocked, her bony back turned to the breeze from the window. She looks good for a woman into her fifties, tall, beautifully made-up, the only flaw a faint sweat stain running through her foundation from her temple to the base of her ear. She's on a roll, naming men, one after the other; this one small and slow, this one overweight and wise. She'll go on until she's stopped.

Ruby, blousy, sad Ruby, is on the floral couch, near Dutch, and she's made a nest for herself, fluffing her gown and tucking the paisley cushions around and behind her. She's well on her way to oblivion. She looks like the Maja would look had Goya poured her a drink and asked her to sit up a little.

I've opened the windows on either side of the fireplace to get some cold air in off the lake. What air there is hits each of us separately, cutting through the leaden heat we've been fighting all afternoon with cold champagne and a swim and this ratty Japanese fan.

It's July and no-one was born in July but we're together, and we've already pretended it's December and March and May.

The cake, on the pine table between us, is covered with dozens of multi-coloured candles, all of them charred and leaning. We've each taken a turn making a wish, stopping to relight the candles every time, and no-one has told. I have no idea why I ordered such a big cake, as if there were still sticky children to hover around it and ask for a third piece before climbing onto the closest lap. There is an empty champagne bottle, a dead soldier as Dutch calls them, on the floor under the table and another nearly dead one in her hand but the cake sits almost whole, plump and pink and messy with candle wax. Our three slices have made hardly a dent.

Dutch moves around the couch to sit down beside Ruby, who puts a long manicured hand on her knee, unable to resist, in spite of the heat, the possible comfort of skin against skin. "I'm lost again," Ruby says. "I've got it straight until John and Boston the year before last. Start there again."

Dutch heaves a melodramatic sigh and begins to recount the intervening men. It's always Ruby who needs to be updated on her exploits. I take no pleasure from her men. They do move into my mind, though without much force. I remember them the way I remember some of her silk dresses, or her silver bracelets. I'm not jealous. Up until David's death I had always been, as I tell them whenever it comes up, well taken care of. And since, well nobody knows about since.

"Let's go down to the beach," I say. "Let's get some air."

"Yes," Ruby says. "I'm feeling a bit boozy. How long have we been sitting here?"

"Three hours," I tell her.

Dutch arches and runs a hand through her hair, lifting it from her neck. She is aware of my impatience with Ruby's need to know about the men, and with her own need to tell. And she tries not to push me. The day of her first divorce, when she made the vow about the lovers, loudly and publicly, in that little restaurant on Broad Street, she pushed me. We had more than enough on her to edge her out of the circle. She brought her face close to mine over the salads, she's always used her face that way, as part of her arsenal, and she said, "Don't you lecture me. I'm going to be fine." She moves Ruby's shoulders away from her own and stands to stretch her legs and back. I don't know if she's fine.

I lead Ruby through the kitchen, stopping at the row of hooks to grab a jacket for her, to cover the flimsy lavender gown she insists on wearing. Dutch is pulling a big, dark sweatshirt, she doesn't ask whose, over her head and down over her sundress. I think about changing out of my cut-offs and decide against it. Cold legs will be a treat. I've just started to wear shorts again after twenty years and I get by quite nicely in town, though I paid the price this afternoon, when I met them at the airport. They came off the plane arm in arm, raving about the duck they'd had. Dutch said it was steak or duck and who wants steak when the smell of duck is in the air. Then they had their say about the cut-offs. I'm hardly offensive in them. My flesh has diminished if anything, as if my body wanted to quiet itself.

Dutch has never stopped wearing anything. She's still thin as a model, long-boned. Ruby is the lush one. She's always been the one with the kind of body men mean when they say body and she's never been above a bit of flaunting, to remind us.

She eases the jacket zipper shut, flattening her abundance as she goes and then she turns to find Dutch, who is already out the door and into the sand, ahead of us. "Why the hell can't you ever wait?" she yells. I wonder if the neighbours are enjoying this.

"Take it easy," I tell her, opening the screen door, guiding her out.

Ruby was thirty-six when Jason rode his new red ten-speed bike into the intersection. She's been a bad drunk ever since. To her credit, she doesn't drink much except when she's with us, or so she says, and I have no reason to think she lies. A good drunk every few years, and then she sobers up after a long night's sleep, whether we're here at the cottage, or at Dutch's or in a hotel. We never go to Ruby's house for our reunions, her husband doesn't want us there. He said, the one time Ruby asked, that it would be too much.

She knows it doesn't matter what she says or does or how she needs us. Her loss is familiar; you know that loss, or its shadow, the minute a child is born. She says she's been weakened, suddenly, irrevocably. She says that's exactly what happens to people, like a car that's been half-demolished. Though sometimes she talks about an old self. Neither Dutch nor I ever hint that she should buck up and count her blessings. She's counting. And she takes our indulgence with the same greed that makes her drunk.

She talks about her other kids more than she would had Jason's skull not been shattered; she knows more about their lives because she doesn't have his. She says they keep her busy. She says her husband still reaches out to her in the morning. She said once, in front of a roaring fire here at the cottage, that she thought ecstasy was a trick the brain plays, like the loss of consciousness. We didn't try to argue with her.

Sometimes we have to put her to bed, pulling the blankets up to her shoulders. Sometimes she tells us that he's supposed to be alive, that he was supposed to bury her. And we watch, until she passes out safely.

The beach is wide this year. Rocks usually covered or half-covered sit exposed, left behind under the moon. We walk separately, scattered over the sand.

Dutch is closest to the water. "Let's find some driftwood," she says. "To keep, here at the cottage. Let's find the perfect piece for each of us."

I can no more resist than walk on my hands. "Ah, metaphor," I say. "Your poet joins us on the beach. He was a poet, wasn't he, the last one?"

Dutch turns her face to the water. "He teaches poetry," she says. "And he's a critic. Writes a little, on the side."

"Erotica?" I ask. "Dedicated to you?"

"No," she says. "He's a highly disciplined intellectual." She picks up a piece of angular wood and fires it into the lake, adding, "At his typewriter."

Ruby stumbles up to her. "He was the most recent one?" she asks.

"Second last," Dutch answers. "You've both forgotten my student, my bright strong boy."

"And the grand total is forty-nine," Ruby says. "That I remember because it's Anne's age. It should be Anne's list shouldn't it? Then it would all work out."

Ruby is taunting. Dutch's vow, made that lunch after her first divorce, had been to take one lover for each year of her life. She's never quite caught up.

"You're still short five," Ruby says. "Five's the magic number, so to speak." Dutch ignores her, bending over to inspect another piece of driftwood. Ruby turns to me. "There must be something we can do?" she asks.

"Nothing I can think of," I tell her. "It's possible for people to be happy with what they've got. Or had, in this case."

"There's always the old dinner party," Ruby stares out over the water. "Maybe at Christmas, at your place, or mine."

"I don't think so," I tell her.

Dutch stands up straight and drops the driftwood she's found. "I think we're talking territory here, Ruby. I think maybe Anne's been casing her own territory. I bet I couldn't get near it."

I fake surprise and am immediately sorry. Dutch has the instincts of a cobra. She's half sure now and that will be enough to keep her going. "Territory," I try. "As if we run on four legs with our bums in the air."

Ruby responds, laughing, loving anything crude. But Dutch doesn't move. It didn't work.

We talked about David's death over the first bottle; I've already shared some of the particulars: the choosing of the coffin, my unwelcome and absurd insistence that they take the dress socks I'd brought with the suit and shirt and tie, his leaving enough for the kids to finish university properly and for me, if I work part time, which we agreed would be best for me. I haven't told them how I miss the feel of his voice moving over my flesh. Or about the new voice beginning to move over it. And I won't.

— 4 —

Neither Dutch nor Ruby came to help bury David. Dutch was in France with someone and I told Ruby that she shouldn't bother to come. It was for the kids and me to manage on our own. There were hundreds at the funeral and more than I can remember at the house after, but they were there because they knew David and cared for him, not for me. I had to hold more than one of them. The kids and I existed on a separate planet that day and for months to follow. And it felt like the place to be.

They both wrote, Ruby's letter full of feeling and warning and small hints, Dutch's an arrogant statement of belief, that I could go on, and would, that I'd had myself a man like few others and now he was gone. That his loss would be as much my companion as his presence. And that she loved me. She didn't indicate this in the closing, but in the body of the letter, as a fact among other facts.

Ruby has joined the driftwood game. She's found something she fancies and has staggered into the lake to hold it under and wash the sand from it. The hem of her gown floats out around her, dark purple on the water. I want to tell her to come out, I can't stand this moving back and forth from the sand to the water, as if they were the same. I imagine walking in with my sandals on, the cold water ruining the leather, seeping between my toes. Water is too much, you can't turn away from it the way you can the sun, or the wind, saving something at least. "You'll ruin that gown," I yell.

She comes out and brings the piece over to me. I recognize what she has seen in it. It's a long bumpy thing and it resembles a backbone, a very strong, shiny backbone. "Her strength of character," I say. "Her famous stamina."

Dutch kicks her way through the small waves toward us. She takes the wood from Ruby and tries to break it over her bent knee. When it won't break, she tucks it into her pocket. "Yes," she says. "Thank you." She pulls something out from under the sweatshirt.

The piece is small and bird-like. There are two extensions which do in fact look just like wings and the head is perfectly rounded and erect. "There are no tail feathers," I say, stupidly.

"Fair enough," Ruby says.

"Oh, I'm sorry," Dutch says. "I just got carried away. We'll find..."

"It's a God damned helpless bird," Ruby says. And then because she doesn't have any choice, and with a practiced nerve in her voice, "I don't mind birds. I like birds."

And she takes off running, lifting her arms and flapping them, leaping drunken little leaps off the sand, wanting laughter.

"We've still got to find Anne," Dutch yells after her. "Get back here and find Anne."

Dutch's first husband, the only one we really knew, divorced her as immediately as he could after finding her with someone in their newly decorated guest bedroom. She had just turned thirty and the kids were napping, likely locked in their rooms. I've always hoped they were. As it turned out her husband had had his dalliances too, and because of the time, and his self-imposed chivalry, he didn't expose her, although she threatened loudly to expose him. She got a decent settlement and her next go round was with an accountant. She's lived moderately well since; she has tenure, and she's travelled, collecting her lovers. She told us she'd need something to do. Over Greek salad, examining her divorced state, that's what she said, "I'll need something to do."

Even then, when we were matrons in our prime, Dutch was the way she'd always be, and Ruby too, asking, while the waiter poured our tea, "So what's the count to date?" Dutch had some catching up to do then, at thirty-one. She stirred honey into her tea and told us what she liked best was the early feeling, when friendship and lust fall all over each other, and that she intended to have a lot of it. Ruby said it sounded like fun.

The words promiscuous and lonely crossed my mind. Why would anyone give up on monogamy, the sheer luxury of it? Why couldn't she at least try? It won't surprise me if we have to hear, one day, about some long-ago wound, something that keeps her moving from one to another, counting. I'm half ready for it all the time. But I won't judge her. Not because I'm the kind of woman who is too ready to understand and forgive. I believe she accepted some kind of touch from David, and I won't forget; I just don't know how to settle a lasting judgement on a warm body.

I've had attitudes. I've thought the whole thing silly, a ridiculous demand for attention from someone who already gets more than enough; I've even thought her immoral, briefly, when I was trying to decide if David had succumbed to her charms. Occasionally, when I imagine her welcoming another new man, a self-righteous sadness surrounds me and everything I see. To correct this, I tell myself it's something to do, it's something for Dutch to do.

We have to find the last piece of driftwood. I should have looked harder earlier when it would have been for them. Now it has to be me and it will likely be a forced connection, if we find anything at all.

Dutch and Ruby walk in random patterns over the sand, venturing absently into the waves, their heads bent in concentration. Then Dutch lets out a whoop and runs deep into the lake, lowering what she's found and splashing water over it. The sweatshirt she's borrowed is soaked and dark on her back.

"Come see," she yells.

Ruby staggers willingly back into the lake, up to her waist. I watch them struggle in the water like failed disciples, wondering what Christ would say if he showed up in his little fishing boat. Probably, "Good grief, ladies. You've got to take it seriously. You've got to want to." They're leaning into each other, knocking each other off balance and grabbing each other just in time.

"This one's mine," Dutch yells. "This is better for me." She holds the piece up against the sunset for inspection. She wades back toward me, Ruby in her wake. It's a near perfect capital F, on a slant. "For fool," she says. "For fool and frivolous and footloose and fancy."

"And fifty-four," I add. "And something else we're not going to name."

"Yes," she says, laughing, Ruby beside her, bending over double with laughter. "That too. Fifty-four, frivolous, fancy, footloose, foolish..." and she mouths the last word, laughing harder. "You won't catch us saying that word out loud on a beach. Oh, no. Not us. It's a sacred word, and we are, if nothing else, devout."

Ruby stands ankle deep. "My daughters use that word at my dining room table," she says, "over the linen. All it takes is a heated debate. But, you're right. It's not that kind of word for us." She comes out of the water, pleased with herself.

I don't care about the word one way or the other.

"You take the backbone," Dutch says. "The backbone is better for you anyway." And she pulls it from her pocket, tossing it to me.

We take our pieces up to the cottage with us and I build a fire to fight the chill in the air while they change out of their wet clothes. They are in the second bedroom, the one with the bunks, and Dutch is saying she'll take the upper because she never has to get up in the night. We all know there's a good chance Ruby will be sick, horribly, loudly sick, before morning. "There's still no mirror in here," Dutch hollers out to me. "How am I supposed to get ready for bed without a mirror?"

"Use mine," I tell her, and I watch her walk into my room wearing men's pyjamas, her cosmetic bag tucked under her arm. Dutch's idea of sexy has varied over the years and I recognize the current choice. I tried it once. David didn't like it for long. He said he wanted to touch exotic things, and lace, he especially liked to touch lace. The fire snaps and spits against the screen.

Dutch emerges from the bedroom with her make-up stripped and a leather shaving case in her hands. "I was just throwing my things into the drawer," she says. "I wasn't snooping, I swear. But this? What is this?" She extends the case toward me. "I have a feeling it's not David's."

I don't want to get angry. I believe her. She wouldn't search around through my things. She watches for clues, aggressively sometimes, but she doesn't dig through underwear for them.

She leans on the door frame a minute, watching me, and then she moves to the couch. "Ruby," she calls. "It might be time for another bottle of champagne." She traces her fingers over the leather. "Anybody we know?"

Ruby emerges in a thick green robe and joins her, tucking her legs up under her as she sits down. "A man?" she asks. "Oh good. Good for you."

"No-one you know," I tell them.

"Married?" Dutch asks.

"No," I answer.

"Then you might?..." Ruby gives me the opening.

"No, I won't be," I tell them. They're making me feel tight-assed, which is their intention. "He's a dentist," I offer. "He's been divorced for a long time. Not especially rich, or brilliant, or handsome."

Dutch raises her eyebrows elaborately at Ruby. "We know all about not especially handsome," she says. "Handsome is as handsome does. Carry on."

"That's all," I say, and before I can think to stop myself, as if the words have been waiting in my throat, fully arranged, for years, "Nice girls don't tell."

Ruby musters an effort, she tries to help us out of this. "Who knows what nice girls do?" she asks. "We're just glad you've got somebody. Some company or whatever." She leans forward with the champagne and fills our glasses. "We'll drink to him."

Dutch declines the drink and takes a cushion from Ruby's lap. She lifts the cushion into the air, holds it there for a minute, twirling it slowly between her hands and then she throws it at me, hard, aiming precisely, hitting me square in the face. The cushion drops into my lap but I don't touch it.

"You think I've told," she says. "Well you're dead wrong. I've never told. I've named names and places and frequencies but I've never told.'' She pulls another cushion away from Ruby. ''I'll tell you now. I'll tell you that some men make me feel all liquid and beautiful, like I've just crawled out of the sea. I'll tell you that some behave like auto mechanics. And I'll tell you that some make me feel nothing at all, which is, in its way, a hell of an accomplishment.'' She stops, waiting to see if we're going to put up with it. It seems we are. ''Some want comfort, only that, like children with a brightly coloured cookie jar. Some get a little brutal, they hold too hard, or bite too hard, harder than you can stand, and you let them off because it's only a bruise or two, and you can, of course, return in kind. Though not as hard. I never could. And some of them cry, though not necessarily the ones...''

''That's enough,'' Ruby says. She tries to take Dutch's arm but Dutch won't let her have it.

''I haven't had a very successful decade,'' Dutch says. She puts her feet up on the table beside the dried-out cake, pulling up her pyjama legs. ''Look at these gams,'' she says. ''Feast your eyes on these blue babies. I'm old,'' she says. ''I'm done.'' She throws her arms behind her head in an immense theatrical gesture, trying to cut through the sadness waiting for us in the air.

Ruby runs a drunken finger along a large blue vein which extends from Dutch's ankle to her knee, just under the tanned skin. ''I felt sorry for that student,'' Dutch says, ''this spring. I told him he had no business in my bed. He's quite determined to reassure me though. He talks about a body I don't think I've ever had. I don't know what kind of game he's playing.''

''Maybe he loves you,'' Ruby says, and this cuts through it; Dutch and I both throw our heads back and roar with laughter. ''All right,'' Ruby says. ''Maybe he needs you. You specifically. Though I'd argue for love if I thought I had a chance here.'' She pulls Dutch's pyjamas down over her legs. ''You've known all along what you were doing. You've kept busy. Just hang on.''

''Ah, yes,'' Dutch says. ''You're right. I'll just hang on.''

''Yes,'' I say. ''It could be we're too far gone to handle this tonight.'' I lift the cushion from my lap, line it up with Dutch's head and fire it. She turns her face slightly but she doesn't duck.

''I'm not drunk,'' Dutch says. ''Though I'm willing to keep trying.'' She goes to the refrigerator for a fresh bottle. She returns with it and climbs up to stand on the couch, which is soft and giving under her weight. ''One more soldier,'' she says. She holds the bottle between her knees and pulls. ''Shit,'' she says. She tries to ease the cork out with her thumbs but it pops and flies up into the rafters, where it stays, though we all wait for it. Her laughter, when she collapses on the couch, is coarse. Foam flows over her hands as she pours. "I'm glad we drink champagne," she says, "and not just any old wine." She lifts her glass. "Shall we have a toast to nice girls?" she asks. "Who can put it into words?" She stares blankly at me. "You?"

"Put your glass down," I tell her. I have surprised myself; I didn't feel this coming. I could stop it. I know how to stop the gestures freed this way.

She places her glass on the table and crosses her arms. "You'd rather not?" she asks.

Ruby leans over and gathers all the cushions back to her lap, piling them one on top of another.

"Ruby," I ask. "How many lovers do you have in your dark, murky past?"

"What?" she asks.

" 'Fess up," I tell her. "From university. From before you married, when you were working in Winnipeg."

"There was no-one," she says. "Before I was married or after. You should know that." She shifts around on the couch, rearranging her robe under her. "Lord," she says.

"No-one?" I ask again. "Not one little visit in the night?"

Dutch smiles broadly.

"You think my way wasn't as fascinating as yours?" Ruby asks. "You think I've missed something?" She takes one of Dutch's cigarettes from the pack and lights it, pulling the smoke into her lungs and exhaling it with some energy toward us. "I've had my own record to keep."

"And you know as much as I know," Dutch tells her. "All from the same source."

"You bet your ass I do," Ruby says. "I'm not sure you're not patronizing me but I'm damned sure I know as much as either of you."

"I'm not patronizing you," Dutch says, squinting up into the rafters. "I can imagine one man."

"I'm not patronizing you either," I tell her. "That's not the intention."

Ruby pushes the cushions aside and takes one of Dutch's feet onto her lap. She begins to rub it.

"From all the information available," I say, "you have had forty-nine men."

"Correct," Dutch says. "I should have tried harder when I was young. That's what I should have done."

"I'll give you your five," I tell her. I go to a kitchen drawer and find a pad of paper and a pencil which has a yellow tassel hanging from the eraser end. "I've never paid close attention to your men," I say. "Not as close as I've pretended. But we're going to list them, on paper, and I'm going to throw mine in. And we're going to remember everything. Every detail, large or small. And David is not part of the deal."

I walk over to the window. There is a gloss on the water now, the reflected light from all the individual stars enters each wave before it hits the sand. You'd think the details would run together after a while. But they don't. There are always thousands of them.

I close both windows and when I turn around Dutch is hugging Ruby's head to her own. I watch her bright auburn hair cover and mix with Ruby's grey blonde.

Dutch straightens up. "Let's get at it," she says.

"Ruby," I say. "You don't have to take part if this is going to make you uncomfortable. You can listen."

She breaks her cigarette in half and pitches it into the fire. "I don't want to listen," she says. "You can count me in. I've got details. All sizes."

"Where should we start?" I ask. "Nineteen fifty-four?"

"Earlier," Dutch says. "Fifty-one. We're going to continue to have birthdays, you know. Have you considered that?"

"Not seriously," I tell her. "But I'm not necessarily putting everything on the table now. You could have those veins stripped," I say, "if they're a problem. Which I find hard to believe."

"And my teeth capped," she says. "And my bum tucked. And my hands softened. And my heart freshened right up, good as new. And they can even do things with —"

Ruby throws her hand over Dutch's mouth and they both laugh at the words not said.

I take the cigarette pack and begin to rule the paper, writing nineteen fifty-one in the margin near the top. The lines aren't as straight as they might be. I carry on, drawing long lines down the page, putting one of our names at the head of each column. I have to open my eyes wide. I have to concentrate.

Dutch leans back into the couch, comfortable. She gives Ruby her other foot.

Several horse-flies have discovered the cake. They buzz around it and then the bravest dives right in, sinking into the icing farther than he expected to. He lifts one leg free and then the other and he beats his wings like hell but he's only making things worse for himself. Some of the others land on a crustier surface, where it's safer.

— 11 —

"That's disgusting," Dutch says. She reaches forward and slips her finger under the trapped fly, freeing him, but he's all goo so she dunks him, the lower half of him, into her champagne. He stumbles around on her palm, cleaning his legs as fast as he can and then he's gone. We all watch him soar away.

"If we're drunk," Ruby says, "and I think we are, we'll need some coffee." She sits up and throws Dutch's feet from her lap. "And something else," she says, holding her head the way she thinks a sober woman would. " 'Almosts' count."

I slide the cigarettes back across the table to Dutch. "Well they've always meant the world to me," she says. "We'll mark the almosts with an asterisk. They count for something."

We each have a small sip of what must be the last bottle. In the morning we will be sober again, God willing, and maybe we'll re-arrange the furniture, Ruby likes to do that, or we could drive into town for another part cord of wood.

We may well regret what we're about to do. I can feel it hang-ing in the air over us at breakfast, the regret. I can feel it following us when we separate to dress and make ourselves up.

Ruby is a little jumpy, she's trying to bring some order to the mess on the pine table; she is unsure but game. Dutch rests her head on the back of the couch and closes her eyes; she's already gone, she's in someone's arms.

"All right," I tell them. "It's nineteen fifty-one. And we're all as pure as the driven snow."

Music Lessons

Most of us who grew up in that time, in that place, in that little subclass of well off girls in well off towns seem now to me interchangeable, like foundlings. We all grew around the same rules, the same expectations. Among the many things we did in my town, with a strangely limited variation in skill, was play the piano. We were all taught to play by Mrs. Summers, though I finished with her alone.

The osmosis which is at work among very young women, beginning always with the one who will tell, the one who will act out a scene for friends gathered round her in some flouncy bedroom, was at work among us. The substance of our minds, like the contents of our closets, was swapped and shared in a continuous, generous game. Perhaps, if we had lost our virginity at thirteen, I would have many elaborate scenes in my memory rather than one. Perhaps not. The osmosis thickened and slowed just as the loss of virginity accelerated. But we knew for a time, and were happy knowing, what the world held. I remember knowing what Mrs. Summers would do when I showed up for a lesson sporting my first bra. I remember knowing that when it was over I would be able to sit on the flouncy bed and say, *guess what*. My world and my comfort in it depended on the sharing of events. This is part of the silliness for which young girls are, cruelly, ridiculed.

What Mrs. Summers did was exactly as had been reported. She put her hand firmly on my shoulder and turned me under her gaze like a work of art. "Sweet," she said. "Just sweet." And I felt, as it had been guaranteed I would feel, dumb. The surprise was the kindness in her voice and in her hands. She was encouraging our adolescence when everyone else was extremely busy avoiding it. In her time, she said, girls had been bound tight and flat.

Mrs. Summers had, even into her sixties, elegant sculptured legs and wonderful carriage. She had the good shoulders and the deep full bosom of women who love and manage music. Though she played the organ in the Presbyterian church, she had no affiliation with any of our mothers or grandmothers. She was not a bridge player or a Daughter of the Empire. She did not quilt or make hats or gossip.

Her dark red brick house had a wide front porch and an oak door with three small, uncurtained windows. Before each lesson I would stretch up to those windows and watch her coming to the door. She walked erect, patting her hair to ensure that no grey blonde strands had escaped the chignon, straightening her gown; it was always a gown, full and rich with colour. And always, just before she put her hand to the knob, she prepared a smile. With the swing of the door came a rush of smells: furniture polish and perfume and smoke from the fire in the winter. And her voice, across the threshold, "Elizabeth dear," as if surprised, delighted.

The piano was a brilliant black, dustless always, with one framed picture sitting on top, of the two of them, Mrs. Summers and her husband, standing under a grapefruit tree, in the south. I could always feel Mr. Summers in the house when I took my lesson, though he never coughed or answered the phone. He was not seen in church either; if he liked music his taste did not run to hymns or to the plunkings of adolescent girls. They had no children, only a Scottie dog and a vegetable garden.

Each spring he could be seen painting the red front porch steps, alternately, so his wife's students could still get in to her. He would stand back beside his paint can, the brush in his hand and watch us leap up the steps, giving no instruction, trusting our good sense.

Within hours of his death, the doctor's wife let it be known that Mrs. Summers had found him slumped at the sweet pea fence. He had been tidying them, arranging them through the wire. People said he had only a few yards left to do, as if that signified injustice.

His funeral was a big one. He had been the hardware man and a councillor and years before he had bought the Scouts four big tents which were still in use. It was my first non-family funeral. I was determined to go, as were all my friends, because we wanted to see how Mrs. Summers would grieve.

She grieved at her usual place, at the organ. The front row of the church was filled with his people, brothers and nephews and nieces and a few strange children, but she did not take her place with them. She stayed at the organ throughout the service, playing the music or staring at it. I was smart enough to know that she was expressing something through the music but it was nothing I could recognize, nothing I had been exposed to in her living room.

I knew only that the level of difficulty was beyond her audience, had likely been pulled up from her time as a young woman at the conservatory. Toward the end of the service she switched to the chimes, making herself heard throughout the town and into the countryside. I imagined a farmer, not far away, walking across a yard with a cream can in his hand, pausing, his movement stopped by the chimes. After the service the word "appalled" moved through the circles of people standing on the sidewalk and on the grass. My friends and I were not appalled, we were thrilled.

It was assumed that lessons would stop for at least a while but Mrs. Summers put out a few phone calls and said no, there would be no interruption. As I took the steps up to my lesson a week later I wondered about them, wondered who would paint them. I decided I would. I would get my dad or my brother to help me or I would do it alone, in the spring, when I could be sure the memory of the painting wouldn't hurt her. I didn't tell my friends about this plan; they would have wanted to join me, to help. I wanted it to be a small thing, a quiet private thing.

I had checked with my mother about what to say to Mrs. Summers, not sure if I should say anything at all.

"Just keep it simple," she said. "Just say you are sorry."

"How should I say it?" I asked.

"Well, are you sorry?" she asked. "Did you like him?"

"Yes."

"Then don't worry." As usual her help, her preparation, her warning, was unadorned. It seemed inadequate when compared to the enriched and detailed advice of my friends, who had rehearsed their sympathy.

As Mrs. Summers approached the door I repeated under my breath, I'm sorry, I'm sorry. The smile she prepared was not the same as the old smiles. She opened the door and I said it aloud just at the moment she was saying my name. I didn't know if she'd heard me.

There was some concern about the vegetable garden that fall but she managed it. It was almost as well tended as it had been. My friends and I saw her when we were riding past on our way to school, stooped low in the varying greens of the garden, bright and undaunted in her yellow pedal pushers and grey sweatshirt. She wore gloves to protect her hands.

The first change came a few weeks later, when the garden was finished. On the piano, beside the Florida picture, sat another, younger picture. She was not a bride, was something between a bride and a Florida woman, perhaps thirty. Mr. Summers was slim and grinning and turned away from her as if talking to someone just outside the camera's range.

The following week the picture I had been hoping for was there. She was a bride, though not in white, like my mother. She wore a tailored suit and a wrist corsage and spectator shoes, black and white or navy and white. Her left hand was held in such a way that her ring picked up the sunlight of the wedding day. He wore a suit with wide lapels and wide stripes and a felt hat tipped forward, on an angle across his face. His arm was wrapped around her waist, his hand flat on her stomach. I liked these pictures, liked their arrangement on the piano, facing me.

When the other pictures appeared on the opposite side of the piano, in grey cardboard frames, five of them, I forgot good manners and stared boldly. There were five men, all young. One leaned against the flank of a Clydesdale, his hands in the pockets of his draped pants. One knelt in a soldier's uniform beside a dog. Two others, though not alike, leaned in a shared pose against the hoods of large dark cars. And one of them, with the unmistakable jaw and the eyes I saw every day in the mirror, was my grandfather.

"Lovers," she said. "They're just my lovers, dear."

She was not with any of them.

Word got out, of course. Lovers on the piano. It wasn't good. Soon music students were taking the longer walk across the tracks to the new high school teacher who, it was said, was just as qualified, if not quite so experienced.

I didn't take the longer walk. My mother was puzzled; I saw her on the phone, listening, and I knew she was puzzled but she shook her head. "No," she said. "No. I won't be taking Elizabeth away from her."

I didn't ask my mother why she insisted that I continue with Mrs. Summers and though it's too late now, I still wonder how the characters arranged themselves in her head that fall. My friends hounded me for a while about the lovers, about the possibility of deeper, darker things, eager for oddity at least, if not perversity. But something stopped me from acting out the small things I saw. I was not puffed up with knowledge, did not feel unique and envied; if they had sensed any of that they would have sliced my fingers off at the knuckles, ending my music lessons forever. I felt alone and terrified.

Mrs. Summers struck my hands with her crossword puzzle book just after Christmas. I remember the mantel was still draped in garlands and the reindeer stood precariously on the snow-covered mirror on the buffet. I hadn't practised much during the vacation;

my pieces were weak. Perhaps, knowing I was the only student, I wanted to feel a bit of power over her. She was sorry immediately, or seemed to be, but the next week she rapped my back with her knuckles, telling me to sit up straight, sit erect. Her gowns were no longer starched and crisp, the chignon was gone. Her hair hung loose and coarse and long. Eventually she sat in the brocade chair by the window, leafing absently through old photograph albums while I played. This arrangement suited me but I knew I wouldn't pass my examination without her help. I wanted to play the piano well, perhaps thinking this would please her, in spite of everything.

I knew about winter by then, how it works on women. My father joked secretly about my mother's February moods, telling us not to take things to heart, that spring would bring her back to herself. I hoped spring would work for Mrs. Summers too.

But when it came, when the snow moved in dirty chunks down the street, carried by the run-off, things were worse. Mrs. Summers hadn't helped me at all; my mother seemed oblivious to my flounderings on the piano at home and my friends said they were far ahead of me. The day of my last lesson Mrs. Summers didn't prepare a smile at all and she looked back at me through those three small windows in the oak door. I was bent down unlacing my saddle shoes when I noticed the navy and white spectators from her wedding day. She lifted her dingy gown.

"Remember these?" she asked.

"Yes," I answered.

She wheeled her back to me, going to the piano bench. "Of course you don't," she snapped. "How could you?" She sat down and played for me, pieces I had not even imagined. She began to hiss at her blue-veined fingers as they missed their place, their time. When the half-hour was up she named a date for my examination. We both knew there was little chance I'd pass.

I could have told. I could have given the details to my mother and to my friends, who would have confided in their mothers. I could have lied myself into the glory of victimization. I'd done it before. But I was drawn to the hurt, to the chaos. There was an odd comfort in me. I wondered if I was making what my mother had once called a moral choice, a choice that would make my life easier, or harder.

The steps had always been blood red. I charged the paint and the brush to my father's account at the hardware store and I took our broom over with me and a rag I had soaked with the garden hose. I cleaned the steps and painted every other one, just as Mr. Summers had. She didn't come out that first day but on the second day I had just dropped everything and begun to wipe the steps again with my rag when the oak door swung open.

"Will you just go away?" she said. "Just disappear."

I held my ground, stood erect with the rag dripping at my side. She watched the tears, unstoppable, sliding down my cheeks. I didn't wipe them away or take the deep breath that brings pride back.

She came at me with her arms out and though there was no way to tell whether she was going to pound me or lean on me or hug me, I could not have run. Her hands were firm on my shoulders; the sound she made was loud and brutal and almost young.

The Replacement

I moved into the big bedroom when my brother left home for university; I was thirteen. Miss Dickson moved in with our next-door neighbour, the widowed Mrs. Dunn, a few months later. Her bedroom window, a movie screen rectangle, faced mine above the blue snow-covered lawns. She had drapes, pink and black, flamingos in a dark swamp, and there was an orange blind as well, a second assurance of privacy, but she never pulled the drapes and I could watch her easily through the ancient blind, watch her silhouette, slightly enlarged, her angles, slightly distorted.

She had been hired midway through the year to replace the teacher whose steady pouring hands we had reduced to clumps of quivering nerves. When she came into the chemistry lab, that first time in January, it was clear we wouldn't be reducing her to anything. She walked back and forth across the front of the room, walked toward us and among us with a detachment and an odd smile that promised nothing. She certainly wasn't friendly. The only friendly teachers were the youngest, most awkward ones. She was more like a competent machine, with just a hint of lustre.

Her suit was grey that first day, with narrow lapels and a walking slit part way up the back of the skirt. And she had what I've come to know as a good haircut. Her hair was the same every minute of the day, a light auburn falling just so. It was only after she took off her jacket, only after I saw the glorious silk print that lined it, all oranges and yellows and mauves, only then did I look at her face and see that she was beautiful. And I saw that she didn't know she was beautiful, or if she'd known, had forgotten.

Because Miss Dickson was so easily perfect, I couldn't look at her without seeing myself standing beside her. I began to despise my twister ankle socks and my hot pink pleated neck scarf and all the other evidence of the monstrous effort put into my appearance. Effort sustained by junk-filled closets, half open drawers and a room littered with fads, each new one pushing the old ones deeper into forgotten corners. I stayed as far away from her as I could and I never, ever asked a question.

But I watched her with a passion. I wanted at my fingertips all the information, all the details that worked together to form such a woman. Each night, all that winter and spring, I gathered my books together and trudged upstairs, confusing my parents with this new-found dedication. I arranged everything in a precise muddle on my desk in case I should be caught by my mother, and I watched Miss Dickson as she sat across the way at her window, behind the blind.

For the first hour, that first January night of watching, she worked on her daybook. I was impatient for her to finish. I wanted her to do something real, maybe change into a peignoir, or pluck her eyebrows, or file her nails, anything at all to preserve and perfect what she was. But she didn't. She got up and moved away from the window and then the bathroom light came on. The bathroom window was small and high and heavily frosted; it was impossible to see anything. When she came back to her room, she wore a bulky robe and she sat down at her desk again. She worked for a while and then suddenly closed her daybook, grabbed the pen from her mouth and threw it against the blind. Then she put her hands into her hair and she wrecked it. She moved to her closet, bent over into it and returned to the desk with a flask, just like the one my uncle carried inside his coat, and she drank from it, like a harlot, a delicate harlot. The windowpane was cold and damp on my forehead.

By the end of the second hour, Miss Dickson was barely able to throw off the robe and climb into bed. I was awake in my own bed for a long time, thinking I'd just seen what my mother quietly called a breakdown. She would not be in chemistry class the next day at all. She would still be in a drunken stupor, or on the train, gone off somewhere, lost to me.

But she was there the next day, exactly the same as she'd been the day before. The only change was the colour of the suit; it was tan. The same cut, the same style, but tan. And again when she took her jacket off and put it over the chair at her desk, the lining made me catch my breath. There were circus scenes, circus animals, doing wonderful circus things.

That day after school I went to my mother's closet and found her suits, lifted the jackets away from the hangers and examined the linings. They were all silk, the same as Miss Dickson's, but plain, navy blue, or brown. My mother came into the bedroom and asked what I needed with her suits and I explained about Miss Dickson's jackets. She laughed and said Miss Dickson likely made her own clothes and chose the material for the linings just to perk herself up a little. She asked why it mattered and did I want to learn to sew.

There were three more suits, navy, brown and black and I studied the linings and kept track of them. The only one I didn't like was red and pink, with large distorted faces, the noses and mouths and eyes all out of place. I thought she'd gone too far with that lining and I tried to avoid looking at it.

The drinking continued and I worried. I watched closely every night, afraid she might be caught by Mrs. Dunn, or pass out with a cigarette going and set her room on fire, be burned to death. And I imagined her coming to school some morning still drunk, being fired in the hall in front of everyone by our bald little principal. But nothing happened. She was less delicate in the way she handled the flask, that was all. All through January and February and March she just kept wearing those suits with the beautiful linings and becoming less and less delicate with the flask.

Then in April my mother was at a tea with Mrs. Dunn and learned that Miss Dickson's brother was coming to visit her. He was supposed to be from Montreal and Mrs. Dunn was always, my mother quoted, delighted to get a chance to meet with someone from one of the larger cultural centres. My mother said he was likely a sanitation man, said that's what they called them in the larger cultural centres and wouldn't Mrs. Dunn learn a lot. Reverence for the unknown was not one of my mother's qualities.

The brother was to come on a Sunday and I watched Miss Dickson all the nights leading up to that Sunday, hoping she might straighten around for him. Because she was beginning to spoil herself. Thick creases were forming across her forehead and dark purple shadows were deepening under her eyes. But she didn't let up. She was constant against the orange of that blind, smoking, messing up her hair, pulling on the flask and dropping clumsily on the bed to sleep. I was even getting some homework done, it was so much the same every night. And I was angry. I was nearly ready to ask for my own blind so I wouldn't have to see any more.

When the Sunday came, Miss Dickson sat on Mrs. Dunn's verandah, waiting. I sat on our verandah, my feet propped up against the cement railing and my chemistry book prominently displayed against my legs. Miss Dickson had a book open on her lap too but I could tell she wasn't reading it.

The warm air had already taken the winter smell away and it made me want to be older. It made me wonder if there would ever be a spring when I could understand someone like Miss Dickson and maybe help her somehow. I didn't think about talking it all over, the way my mother sometimes did with one of her old friends. I thought about walking with her, just walking, with some kind of magical caring passing from me to her under the maple trees.

When the car finally pulled up to the curb there were two men in it, not just her brother. As soon as she saw them, she stood up and headed back across the verandah to the front door, but Mrs. Dunn was there, just coming out, and she was trapped. The man who looked like Miss Dickson took the verandah steps in two leaps, went right to her and hugged her. But she was stiff against the hug and kept her head turned away from the other man, the blond one.

He was bearded and as beautiful as she was. He wasn't handsome like the goons in the movie magazines, he was just there, just perfectly there in his big blond way. He watched Miss Dickson in her brother's arms and waited. And the way I loved her finally defined itself in his face. He was what I wanted her to have.

Mrs. Dunn sat them all down and served tea and cupcakes. Miss Dickson was beside her brother with her hand tucked under his arm, staring at the maple trees which were just coming into bud along the street and occasionally looking over at me. She was fidgety and I had the feeling that she might stand up at any minute and call me over.

When Mrs. Dunn finally left them, collecting her china and her teapot and disappearing into the house, Miss Dickson's brother got up and followed her in. I thought maybe I should go into my own house but I resisted. They could ignore me, surely; I wouldn't matter at all, it was so strong between them. They could talk low so I couldn't hear. I had to see him touch her.

When the blond man did touch her, Miss Dickson let out a soft ugly scream and she backed up against the railing, her hands in front of her, pushing against him. And they didn't talk low. He talked about Jan, about things being finished with Jan, about a baby being lost. Miss Dickson just kept yelling that was too damned bad, too damned bad.

I could not have moved if I'd been ordered to. I sat there and willed it to end and it did end soon. Miss Dickson went into the house and the blond man got into the car and sat there until the brother came out and they drove away. I was alone on the street with only the muffled sounds my mother made inside the walls of the house. And the word that came to me was stupid. How stupid they all were, to take something perfect and beautiful and ruin it. And her especially. Didn't she know? Didn't she know what she was? A beautiful man loved a beautiful woman, just as you would dream he might. And it wasn't any good. I blamed everybody, even the lost baby, but it was her I was hardest on. I thought she could have loved him. I could have loved him.

She stopped drinking after that Sunday. Some nights when she was finished with her daybook she actually did file her nails or pluck her eyebrows. I already knew how to do my nails and I'd already decided never to pluck my eyebrows and I was disappointed that nothing magical was going to come to me through that window. In May, my mother fixed her up with one of my father's partners. I couldn't help but see him call for her. My friends at school thought it was all so romantic and they pumped me for information, but they didn't get any. Once, she went for a walk with my mother.

There was no sudden engagement to the young partner, though they seemed to be having a great time whenever I saw them together. Miss Dickson gradually appeared a little healthier, the suits continued in rotation, and I learned a bit about chemistry.

In June, when it got really hot, she pulled her blind up and opened her window. I decided to move my desk; I didn't like being so exposed. I was standing, gathering everything up so I could pull my desk away from the window and I looked over, one last time. She stood at her own window, arranging herself so that she stood exactly as I stood, moved as I moved, putting her arms, her head, everything in the same position as mine. Then she waved and made a signal for me to wait, turning to get something from her dresser. She came back with a lipstick and she wrote a message on her window, backwards, so I could read it, in large block letters. It said I LOVE YOU TOO. Humiliation, immediate and deserved, started to move through me, but the words absorbed the humiliation in a way I still remember more exactly than any chemical experiment.

I wanted very badly to write something back to her but I didn't yet have a lipstick on my dresser and my mind felt stalled, emptied of everything but the message on the glass and the warm spring smell in the air.

I watched from our verandah when her brother came to pick her up at the end of the year and she waved to me as she approached the car, an ordinary friendly wave which caused her brother to turn and look and wave to me too. My mother was with Mrs. Dunn on her steps; I remember her untying her apron and folding it in embarrassment, tucking it under her arm.

I'm teaching in a city now, French, not chemistry, and I've come home with my husband to spend Christmas with my family. I'm not surprised to find my room has changed. The blue dotted Swiss curtains are washed out to near grey; the desk is small. Even my window is smaller than I remember it. I stand looking across the blue snow-covered lawns that separate my parents' house from Mrs. Dunn's. She still boards teachers; I hear the current one is a man, a very nice man from one of the larger cultural centres. I see the faded orange blind has been replaced with white venetians. The boarder thinks he's pulled them shut but thin yellow strips of light, parallel rows of them, escape. And there is a glow behind the blinds, a tantalizing glow. I sit down to wait, aware that I am framed in light against the winter night and its darkness.

Grizzly Mountain

She was to leave on Monday. He would help her pack and carry her bag down to the hotel. He would load her into the beat-up station wagon that took people into the city and close the door on her, likely carefully and without much force. He said it was right that she should go through the physical act of removing herself from him. He said it would help if she could put a distance between them, said it was healthy. He had already put his distance there.

But he said they might as well go on Saturday's climb as planned, as promised. The exertion would be a cleansing. She allowed him these pronouncements because she knew she would think of him for a long time and it would be useful to think of him sometimes as a pompous ass.

They had lived in the small mountain town for almost two years. It was a poor town but so isolated that those who lived there were allowed to forget their poverty most of the time. The people had no compelling past, talked not about themselves as they sat in the hotel beer parlour but about the ones who had deserted when the mine shut down years before and about the ones who had drifted in and out of town since. He was there to teach their kids in the prosperous looking old school; she was there to be with him.

They had climbed the mountain before, in the winter. They'd had cross-country skis and good boots to change into when they'd had to leave the skis behind at the base of the mountain. It had been fine between them then. He smiled whenever he looked at her on that climb, his face seemed to take the smile from her and hold it after he turned away. She knew she was strong and beautiful. Now that he didn't find his smiles in her, she felt something less than strong, something less than beautiful.

The boy had been promised the climb. He was one of the man's students, a small tight boy with beige hair and beige skin and eyes as blue as the lakes that could be seen from the top of the mountain, after the climb. And he had shadows drifting across his eyes, like the clouds drifting in reflection across the lakes.

The boy worshipped the man. It was good clean worship, full of imitation and quick grins. The boy's father had been one of the men who had left the town when the mine closed. He had neither returned nor sent for his family. The boy didn't speak of his absent father and she suspected it was because he had learned, quite bravely, to live with the unspeakable. She often thought when she looked at him that she could kill a man who left a child. A man who could turn his back on that kind of love had nothing to do with life. A man like that was an aberration.

It took no particular effort to include the boy in their lives; he was just quietly there with them, leaving at night to go to his bed as a child of their own might have done. He hadn't been told that she was leaving. He would know on Monday. She thought maybe her leaving would clear some space for him around the man, maybe even please him. There was certainly no need to exclude him from this last climb. Nothing meaningful would be said. She knew the danger of trying to say things for the sake of memory. There would be no closing ceremony.

They packed their gear the night before the climb, packed the food in the morning, after breakfast. They would have cheese and salami and molasses bread for lunch and cold chicken later in the evening, at the fire. And wine, though it made her sneeze. It was one of the things that got under his skin, her sneezing over a glass of fine wine. They often took some with them on small hikes out to one of the lakes where they could be alone, where they could claim all the space around them, miles of it. He needed that much space and he loved the wine then. The sneezing had overtaken her on one of their first hikes, with the Riesling; he'd looked aghast, said it was like farting in a cathedral. She had no particular respect for cathedrals. In retrospect, she began to recognize his comment as the sign that there would be things about her which he would not forgive.

But he was a good friend to her in their sagging bed and on the mountain wildflowers and on the stony beaches. He said she was the space he needed, she was distance, said he could be in her without being aware of her breath on his neck. She didn't care about definition, only hoped she could always be distance, if that was what he loved.

When it was time to set out in the morning, the boy was at their door with his packsack, ready. He offered no hints of manhood. He was graceful and confident, had not yet begun to stretch and stumble. She had seen him swim nude many times and he was hairless, his skin innocent and fresh in the sun. And he took her own nudity with just a slight puzzlement. She was confident she did not exist in his dreams.

He helped her fasten her packsack, gave the man a fake punch on the shoulder and they started out away from the town. When they were nearly at the end of the main street, where the wild country took immediate control, the man who ran the coffee shop waved and hailed them, quickly put a half dozen warm cinnamon buns in a bag and gave it to them, as he had on other mornings when they were setting out. He had been a friend of the boy's father, years before.

They didn't talk as they walked, even the boy didn't need talk. They went quietly deeper into the wild landscape, the distance. Before her time with him, it would not have seemed like distance at all. Distance was uninterrupted, immeasurable, it was snow blankets tucked securely across the prairie, the mildest curve of hills almost immodest. This place was unsettled, flamboyant. The land seemed actually to move as you watched it. It climbed uncontrolled toward the clouds, climbed till it was clear of the trees, threw itself over the top of mountains, eager for valleys. It split itself into streams at their feet, gathered together again to hold arrangements of wildflowers and scrub.

The boy sometimes went on ahead of them, blazing a new trail with the hatchet the man had given him for his eighth birthday. Sometimes he strayed behind them. She sensed he did this so he could have them framed against the dark growth through which they were climbing, as in a picture. Occasionally he would hustle up to her if there were rocks to manage or a stream to jump across, would take her hand in his small one, like an escort.

They were two hours reaching the top of the mountain and they were greeted by deer scrambling over the far edge, giving up their territory, as they always did. The deer would be back, though they would not come close.

The three of them set up camp together, establishing a place for the fire, putting their sleeping bags out, three in a row, gathering twigs and dead grass. They would go back down the side later to collect wood for the fire. She broke open the food pack and started to slice cheese and meat with the fine cool blade of the hunting knife, which the man carried in its sheath on his belt. He'd bought the knife as a present for himself with his first paycheque. He'd come back from shopping with the knife and a shawl for her. The shawl was creamy white with mauve and blue threads woven into the edging. He'd wrapped it around her shoulders and slipped his knife over his belt and they'd sat quietly together in front of a fire.

He had been right about the exercise of the climb. She had forgotten for all that time that she was leaving on Monday. Here at the top of the mountain, eating bread and cheese and meat, she remembered. She thought that if the boy hadn't come, if they had been alone, she might have tried to create a final afternoon. But such a final afternoon would have held chaotic words like sorry and maybe and impossibility. Such a final afternoon would have been like this landscape. She held herself flat and silent, allowed no movement, no shadows. It took all her energy to keep the calm in force.

The man and the boy played chase. They ran over to the small lake near the far edge and threw themselves on the grass, rolling over and over, yelling and laughing, uninhibited, free of all restraint but gravity. She knew they would leap off the mountain without hesitation if not for that one unavoidable pull.

They returned to her and they all slept for a while, together in their row of sleeping bags, and when they awoke the deer were back, grazing. The deer stayed this time and the boy began to talk. He talked of an uncle who had a farm in the south of the province and of another who'd once had a fishing boat. They moved from the uncles to other people, the boy anxious to be told of other kinds of lives, other kinds of towns and landscapes. They took him across the Prairies and up across the Shield, around Lake Superior and down into the south where so many people lived, and through Quebec, through maple sugar bushes and small farms, on through the eastern provinces where they tried to imitate for him the way people talked. He laughed hard at their efforts, threw his head back and held his stomach and she wanted to hug him tight to her own. They took him to that other coast with its steep cliffs and its deadly ocean.

And the man took him to England while she prepared their supper, dividing the chicken evenly among them. The boy very quietly, without taking his eyes off the man's face, got a bag out of his pack. In the bag were three chocolate bars and a package of squashed potato chips. She divided the chips, arranging them beside the chicken with the care of a dinner party hostess.

The boy looked at the plates with pride then and gave her one of his best quick grins. He asked if she wanted more wood for the fire and sprinted down over the side to get it. In the boy's absence, the man knelt behind her and put his hand on her back, rubbing the ridges of her spine through her sweater. He lifted her hair and put the cold tip of his nose behind her ear, his teeth on the back of her neck. She continued to divide and arrange, separate and re-arrange. When a shudder twisted down her spine, he lifted his mouth.

After supper they talked of more countries, sharing with the boy all the information they could summon, all they knew about places they'd been and hadn't been. On the return trip he led them, check-ing his facts as he brought them country by country, province by province, back to the fire on the top of the mountain. He said he didn't think he'd like the Prairies much and it made her catch her breath, made her concentrate for a tough minute on holding a placid face.

When the fire went out they stripped down to their underwear and settled into the sleeping bags, leaving the tops unzipped, loose over them. The night air was gently cool. She lay facing the man for a few minutes and he stroked her hair, tried to rub the creases out of her forehead. He said she'd be happier. He made no effort to keep the love out of his eyes and so, enraged, she turned to face the sky. Stars and light won out against the dark space, making it seem more distant than it really was. She turned again then, toward the boy, who was quiet beside her, his breathing regular and peaceful. She turned finally to the distance within her, turned to it for help against the need to fight, the need to stay. She grieved without sound for most of the night. The man did not try to save her from it.

In the morning she woke to the smell of smoke from the breakfast fire and to an overwhelming sense of love being offered. When she came fully awake she recognized the love in the boy, still sound asleep, curled warm and tight against the hollow of her body, his hands, smeared with grime, resting on his ribs. Easing away from him, she was able, for the first time, to imagine herself gone. And she knew how careless she'd been to allow him to come so close.

Joyride

She drives the highway to the lake half dreaming, watching the sun, hoping to catch the exact moment of connection between the warm round base and the flat wheat fields hundreds of miles away on the horizon. It's a game she plays whenever she can. She has always believed there are other people who do it with her, though their horizons would be their own. The grey truck appears from nowhere.

He accelerates and pulls around in front of her and she gives him her full attention, expecting him to pull away and perhaps lift some stones, throw them against her windshield. When he settles in just yards ahead and stays there, she wonders why he has passed at all. Then she sees him grin into his rearview mirror and wave and she knows the signal is not meant for her. The other truck is there, nestled snugly behind her.

The grey truck is old, with rounded edges and high wooden sides, perhaps for livestock, though it seems clean. She thinks the driver might be in his late thirties. His hair is closely cropped, has been recently shaved around his ears and up his neck to expose the two thick muscles running toward his skull. His shoulders are very steady.

The other truck is blue, of all colours, and newer and sharp-edged. The chrome on the grill reflects the sunlight. The driver is fair, his face wide and heavily boned; his passenger has a softer, smaller face.

The boys are out for a ride, she thinks.

She could have waited for morning, as her husband suggested, but she wanted to get to the lake ahead of all the other weekend people. She's not all that comfortable in heavy traffic. She wonders about double clutching and the other tricks; she is sure there are other tricks that good drivers know.

She tries to pass. She pulls out carefully, afraid she might clip the back of the grey truck but she gets clear, out into the passing lane. He simply accelerates and pulls out ahead of her; child's play, she thinks. She doesn't rule out the possibility of trying again.

There is colour in the sky, mauve and pink and orange, swirling together with the clouds, but the source is gone. She ignores the word trapped because she knows where she is and has lots of gas and fairly good tires and the car has never really failed her. She has never had to pull over to the side of any road and wave down assistance. Just to be safe though, she locks all the doors she can; the rear passenger door on the far side is beyond her reach, even after she throws off her seat belt. When she finishes reaching and twisting to get at the locks, she notices laughter and the slapping of shoulders in the blue truck. The muscled driver of the grey truck doesn't move at all and she begins to think of him as a granite mannequin.

A car passes them from the other direction. She digs into her purse for her cigarettes, puts one in her mouth and punches the lighter on the dash. The wide-jawed driver behind her sits up at his wheel and takes a new grip. She feels a bump, and then another bump. They want me to know how much they can see, she thinks, how much they can do. She throws the cigarette to the floor.

She is beginning to imagine things, specific things; she's lost that battle. Rape jumps easily to mind. She imagines a darning needle and strong thread; how she would, if it were possible, sew herself shut.

Dusk has muted the colour in the sky. She puts her headlights on.

Death moves into her imagination much more reluctantly. She has never had so much as a broken arm, has not bled any more than an ordinary person should, small careless gashes that quickly healed over with the simple assistance of cleanliness. She tries to visualize the exact thickness of the skull. A quarter of an inch perhaps? Thicker in places? Thinner? Hard enough to withstand the force of a kick from a man weighing maybe two hundred pounds? Possibly. But not hard enough to withstand dozens of kicks, from several boots, with God knows what kind of force behind them.

She is almost sure they don't have guns; she's seen no racks and handguns are not at all common in this country. There may be knives though, hunting knives or jack-knives with pictures of fish and grizzly bears on the handles. This is insane, she says, aloud. She is pleased with the reasoned tone in her voice.

The blue truck is pulling up beside her now and the passenger leans out his window. For all the softness of his face, his arm is heavily muscled and dark with hair and sun. He does have a knife, though he is not threatening her with it, is very casual in fact, waves it around conversationally. She can't understand what he is shouting at her. When he sees she can't he thrusts the knife up into the air several times. She notices that the blade isn't clean. She shows all the fear she feels and more, trying to appease. I'm scared. You can stop now. You can leave me now. This horrid concentration, this effort to give them what she thinks they need is taking more skill and energy than she imagined she had.

She hates these bastards. She imagines them beaten by fathers in sweaty undershirts; she imagines teachers with rulers and clenched fists. She doesn't care. It's not her fault. She is innocent. A full colour fantasy comes to ease her: there is a crash; they remain in a bloody heap of steel and intestines while she slips free.

The truck moves back into position behind her and she thinks maybe there is another car approaching but it is only a sharp curve in the road and they take it together. They are still miles from the lake, miles from the prairie town settled in the valley cut by the chain of lakes. They have already passed several narrow dirt roads meeting the highway, each one marked by the illumination of a single Department of Highways light before receding back through the dark empty fields, and there will be more. She fights down the image of the nest of people awaiting her at the cottage, husband and children and perhaps a friend, stopped in to welcome her and share a beer. She fights down the image of the girls in their new flannel nighties, playing Scrabble at the kitchen table, of her son being coaxed from his sandbox and hosed down on the deck.

She knows a lot will depend on what kind of men they are. And on the thrill threshold they've established. She knows there is no real way to measure pain, not from the outside. She will whimper and cry, more than she needs to, from the beginning. If they have among them some acceptable level of achievement, she will guess at it and give it to them, whether or not they have earned it.

She has urinated but they can't know that. The smell fills the car and she imagines that it gives an extra edge to her reflexes.

The grey truck is braking now, chugging, forcing her to do the same. The blue truck pulls alongside, ready to show her something else. This time he bends to the floor of the truck and sits up again with his large hand wrapped around the body of a doll. He extends his arm to her. Where the doll's head should be is the head of a cat. She can see dried blood on the chest and shoulders. He is laughing, banging his head against the rear window. She discovers something new in the pit of her stomach and she begins to gag.

The sudden screech of brakes stops the gagging and the blue truck swerves, nearly broadsiding her, and tucks back in behind again. There must be a car this time. She prepares herself. There is a car and it's beside her and gone and she floors the gas pedal and pulls out and around and she is free. She is in the lead, the grey truck not as alert as the blue truck might have been.

She watches in her mirror as the blue truck passes its companion. With any luck she'll be able to stay beyond his reach. There is a shudder moving through the car but she doesn't lift her foot. She can see only what her headlights show her, the dotted yellow line moving ahead and the gravel shoulder on her right. They guide her. She thinks about the RCMP detachment on the main street of the town. She thinks about everyone she's ever cared about, recites their names.

She is across the tracks, past the gas station and she slows finally because she will have to make a turn soon. Down to sixty, fifty, forty. The blue truck is there, right behind her. She makes the turn and the rear end goes out from under her but she has watched "Knight Rider" so often with her son that she knows what to do and she does it well, steering into the skid, straightening. She is on a residential street and is grateful for the street lights and the lawn sprinklers. She takes the last corner. There are no cruisers parked in front of the detachment, no lights in the windows. She goes down a darker block, around and over to the main street, turning in to angle park in front of the pizza place. She thinks she will leap from the car but she stumbles out and walks to the wooden restaurant door. The blue truck has parked across the street and the men are climbing out of it.

In the washroom, she strips off her skirt and panties and rinses the urine away. She punches the hand drier over and over, holding her clothes up to the warm air. When they are nearly dry she remembers herself, realizes how lucky she's been that no-one has come in to see her standing there half-naked. She puts her clothes on. She looks at her face in the mirror and wonders where her make-up has gone. There is nothing left. Three heavily made-up, giddy teenagers come swinging into the washroom, giving her an immediate deference, and she tries to smile at them as she pulls open the door.

In the dining room there are several university students carrying trays of pizza high over their heads. There are children. She can see glasses of chocolate milk, with straws in them.

All three men sit at a table close to the washroom. The one from the grey truck sees her first and he is out of his chair and beside her, pinching her arm. He whispers, "No harm done, eh?"

The other two are watching her, moving spoons slowly through white mugs of coffee, leaning across the table toward each other.

She knows it won't be long until she is with her own people, bathed and cried out and resting. She knows she should act, now, while they are close. She imagines them driving down the highway in some direction. Though she can't name the law they've broken, she is almost sure there is one, and she can hear the statement she'll make composing itself in her head. The dry details will matter to someone and that someone will get in a car and look for the trucks and find them, likely not far away. She will be able to identify them.

She walks into the kitchen. The red-haired waiter, the one the kids like so much, calls her, miraculously, by name. "Do you want Frank?" he asks. Frank is the owner, she thinks. Frank is likely sane. "Yes," she answers.

When he comes through the doors, his dark chin leading his face officiously, she begins to cry, just a little. She can smell her stench rising with the steam in the kitchen and she knows she has not been successful in rinsing the urine out of her clothes.

"You tell me," Frank says. "You tell me what happened." He yells at a waiter. "Get me a glass of cold water here."

She sits where Frank has put her, beside an open back door, sipping at the water the young man has offered. Frank is talking to her, making a point of looking very forcefully at her face, as if this will help. She leans over and turns her head to look out through the door. It's only an empty alley; she can see the decrepit backs of buildings and above them the black prairie sky. Moths thud repeatedly against the bare light bulb above the door and a cold breeze wraps itself around her shoulders.

Women of Influence

We had a fairly good night. My mother's dying is still following its own steady pace but there was pleasure in being together, pleasure even in silence. Last week, when she acknowledged the approach of her death, simply by saying that she didn't particularly want to be alone, my brothers and I arranged to stay with her in her hospital room, day and night. We take shifts and we co-operate with the staff by keeping out of the way and by accepting, or pretending to accept, their professional judgement. It's good that we are all here now, gathered from our separate parts of the country. The four of us are stronger than any hospital administration. We won't leave her.

She's getting notes and letters with her greeting cards; her friends and relatives offer specific, cherished memories. Odd things. Last night my aunt's letter, written in my uncle's hand, brought full colour scenes to her mind; I could see it in her face as she listened to me reading it. Some of the scenes included me, as a child. Many of them gave off-handed praise for my mother's character, which is her due. As I drive across the city to my aunt's hospital, the red sun is just rising. I notice kitchen lights coming on. There have been no other cars, only a snow-plough, gathering the filthy February build up.

My mother's ward is not one of the new ones wherein family responsibility is acknowledged; many of the other patients, who are also dying, see no-one but uniformed staff from one Sunday to the next. Sunday's a big day, containing, as only Sunday could, a compression of anger and guilt and grief and compassion, as if the visitors cannot deny the day its rights. Through the week there are no flower deliveries; night tables hold Bibles and Testaments and discarded reading glasses and pictures of children, some dated, some very recent. The day nurses do not come bustling down the hall with news of the world. The world doesn't exist. Each day is twenty-four hours of bits of sleep and bits of talk and bits of pain.

The cries and moans come at any time though they are harder to ignore in the night. There is no place to look in the night for distraction, no bright roof-tops in the window. Albert, down the hall, is the best we can hope for at night; of all his loud contributions, we favour the scotch-enema story. Before he was admitted, his wife had had to go to an all-night drugstore for an enema kit, her last valiant effort. It cost her nineteen dollars. He said if he'd known, he would have sent her out for scotch. This in a bellowing voice to the young night nurse and down the hall to us. Maybe my mother's last good laugh. She's made me repeat it twice.

There is no spiritual unease in my mother's room and I am immensely grateful. She has always had at her disposal the God she first decided she believed in. I can lift her and turn her, can feed her as patiently as I have fed my babies. I can reach my arms through the steel bars of her bed to rub her small aching legs. I can jump with her to any time she remembers, lying when I have to, but I can do no more. I could not possibly pray.

There is a staffroom down the hall from my mother's and the nurses encourage me to have a cup of tea while they are with her, changing the catheter or checking the intravenous or shooting the pain-killer into her bruised hip. It's easy to tell when the pain is edging back now; I can get her a shot of codeine and have it working before the grimace comes to her face. One of the nurses told us that we are alike, my mother and I, in the face. I squared my shoulders and stuck my nose into the air. My mother lit up a little, not at my acceptance of the flattery, as the nurse might have thought; we are not good-looking women. She brightened at my urge to be an ass, even at her deathbed. It was a little joke.

The morning is coming brighter now. There are cars at intersections, waiting alone against red lights. I can see the silhouette of the other hospital ahead, looming confidently over the wartime houses which surround it. The sun looks strangely red for winter.

There is an old picture with my aunt's letter. They stand together; my mother, twelve or thirteen in a modest dark dress, holds the hand of the brilliantly beautiful younger sister. I have seen the picture before and I've always imagined that my mother had set my aunt's golden ringlets patiently in preparation for the day of visiting and picture-taking. Her own hair is short and dark, a bob, I think. Her face speaks to the camera with the recent acceptance of her fate as a woman: I know I'm plain, it says, but I'm good, just the same. In her letter my aunt speaks of their young sisterhood on the farm, of harvesting crews and eager young men, as if the men were eager for both of them. In the final paragraph, she comes close to what she wants to say: "You always took such care with my clothes and hair. You taught me to be proud of myself."

I wonder if she's pretty in her hospital bed. She is six years younger than my mother, the fact of their ages is mentioned a lot now, but her prognosis is the same.

She had an early influence on me, the result of my frequent summer stays with her on the farm. My parents took motor trips in the summer, to the coast or to Lake Louise and my aunt always asked if she could have me. I went eagerly because I thought I should.

She would have been younger then than I am now. She was tall and forceful, square-shouldered, competent even in bone structure. She taught school; troublesome kids were saved by a year of her care. The men loved her; she was funny and often quoted, and always quoting others, sharing absurdities and telling stories which made other people look good and worth knowing. If things got too settled at a family gathering she would start something or encourage someone else to. "Ray," she'd say. "Tell the kids about Stew Gault and that mare." If she was met with reticence she would start the story herself, with just a few words, tempting the one whose story it was until he could no longer resist and we'd have it. She was a singer of first bars, reminding the singers, setting them off. She wore bright wool dresses with just the right amount of jewellery and sometimes slacks, creased like a man's, like Lauren Bacall's. She wore make-up daily, flaunting dark eyes and bright lips.

She talked to me when I stayed with her and smiled a lot. She had ideas for my hair, would comb through the curly mess over and over and try with pins and ribbons to expose what she said could be a pretty little face. She nagged me to shed the ten extra pounds I carried, fixed me lots of fruit. But I ran whenever I could to my uncle in the fields, carrying cold water and matrimonial squares wrapped carefully in waxed paper. And I cruised the ditches with the Labs, their muscled black bodies eager to help me find whatever it was I hunted. I remember her disappointed face at the table when I asked my uncle for more potatoes and he scooped whatever was left evenly between his plate and mine. She didn't yet have her own daughter.

My mother has been a quieter kind of woman, short and solid, raising her kids in town, away from the dirt and strain of the farm. She did not finish high school, she stayed on the farm to help with the younger half of the family until she married the serious young man one stile away. I do not remember her ever telling a story.

She has always been audience, pure audience. The storytellers, her brothers and friends, measured their skill on her face, working toward the slow sure smile. A very few times, when things were really rolling, a laugh would burst aloud from her and she'd say, "I'd forgotten. Oh, I'd forgotten." When she was made to smile it seemed she had been given something that would stay with her.

She refinished furniture: chairs and trunks and beds. Men from Toronto sniffed her out, offered what she called big prices for the pieces she had stashed all over the basement but she just laughed and gave them coffee and pie, then a motherly pat as she put them out the door. She designed quilts and worked on them in the winter evenings as she watched her hockey games, cheered her Frenchmen down the ice. I have a dozen of her quilts and they are beautiful; my daughters have their own, which I am not to use. She served the people she loved what they craved: hickory nuts in the tarts for John, a good whitefish dinner for Gordon, garden corn for Emily's kids. In her fully modern town kitchen she had bins built for sugar and flour.

In a family crisis, and I mean the big family here, not just us, she would gather people to talk, to see if something couldn't be done. She didn't sit at the table with them, she stood at the counter buttering raisin bread or slicing cake and she didn't offer suggestions, as my aunt did, but it was her table.

When my first university calendar arrived she said, "None of it will do you any harm." The only suggestion I remember, other than the long ago wash your hair kind of suggestion, was when my own first child was born. In a small correct script, on blue scented paper, "Your place is at home with your baby. Don't rush away." This when feminism was already old news. I have followed her advice. My degree is an obscure memory and my kids are solid, though not exceptional in any way. She would think me foolish if I expected them to be.

I blamed her for a time, wished she had come down hard on me, made me into something extreme and wonderful, as my aunt would have. A girl whose mother thinks hair should be nothing more than clean is at a tremendous disadvantage.

The lot here is half empty, parking will not be a problem. I'll sit for a minute and finish my cigarette; there will be oxygen in this room too.

When my brother came into the room this morning, my mother was still holding my aunt's letter, staring carefully at her own thoughts. She didn't acknowledge him. He had taken his boots off at the door and padded around to the other side of the bed, pulling a chair up close to ask what she wanted for breakfast. He always takes the early morning shift and has developed a system to get her what she thinks she might try to eat. The trolley in the hall holds the trays and he lifts each lid silently, switching things as necessary to make her a perfect breakfast. She rarely eats more than half a bite and that only to please him but it's the way their time begins. He is telling her that he would commit grand larceny on her behalf as he sneaks around the grey hospital hallway in his socks.

My mother gave him her just-a-minute face and spoke to me. "I've wasted a lot of time believing that her beautiful face made mine uglier. Now I'm thinking what a pleasure it was to have her all those years. I should have taken her just the way I took a sunset, or a lace tablecloth."

My brother busied himself by rolling up his sleeves, wanting no explanation.

My mother cleared her throat. "Freshen yourself a little," she said. "You look tired."

I walked to the spotless old bathroom and saw in the mirror a tired middle-aged face that did indeed need freshening. I scrubbed my face hard. My brother came in with my purse. "Mom says your make-up is likely in here," he said, shrugging his shoulders. There was make-up in it all right, enough to transform me, blue and red and pink and brown, each in its respective little case, each with its respective little job. I didn't stop at daytime subtlety, I applied and reapplied. I brushed my hair a hundred strokes, watching it snap back as always to disorder. When I presented myself at my mother's bedside, she grinned. Her teeth were dark and her mouth sore from the dryness. "From the day you were born," she said, "I've loved your hair best." She hesitated, then "I'll see you tonight." I kissed her forehead, leaving a bright red lip print. My brother sat stirring her orange juice with a straw.

The corridors in this hospital are wider, brighter. The rugs continue beyond the first floor. I see my uncle sitting alone at the end of a long hall, in front of a window. I approach him, careful not to look into the rooms I am passing. A nurse stops to ask if she can help and I say no. My uncle hasn't heard me so I sit down close to him, wishing I could offer cold water and matrimonial squares, wishing he was young and brown. He looks up with bleary eyes and smiles.

"How is your mother this morning?" he asks. I think this is too much for one man.

"Dan's with her," I tell him. "She's talking a bit."

He shakes his head. It is too much. He clears his throat. "Jo-Anne is coming from Ottawa. She left last night, driving."

Jo-Anne is the daughter who was proper raw material. Even when half-grown she was sociable and elegant, capable. She studied dance at the conservatory in Toronto, was driven hundreds of miles for her lessons. My mother has a picture of her at home; she sits in front of a fire at a cottage in a blue angora sweater, her hand caught in the act of lifting her pale blonde hair away from her face. She studied in France where she met and married a French Canadian composer. I suspect she has magnificent children. I can see that my uncle has been following her in his mind all night, knows within a half-hour what her safe arrival time should be.

"Your aunt has had a bit to eat," he says. "If she's sleeping, you just nudge her a little, she'll want to see you."

I stand up and move into the room. My aunt lies flat out, stiff. Her eyes are closed. Her pain has been more sudden and mysterious than my mother's; it's a different kind of thing. She is controlling herself with the force of her will and I hesitate to touch her. She has not wasted away to seventy pounds as my mother has; she still looks beautiful and almost healthy. A cold compress rests on her forehead. One of her hands is flat on her stomach and the other clutches the sheet. I reach for the hand that isn't clutching. She opens her eyes, perhaps expecting her daughter. When she sees it's me she says my name and closes her hand over mine, sliding them together up to her chest.

"How is your mother?" she asks.

"She's comfortable," I answer, angry. "Can't they give you something?"

She ignores my question. "Is she afraid?"

"I don't think so," I tell her.

"Good," she says, moving her head, with a slow effort, toward me. "Did you read her my letter? I said at the top that someone was to read it to her."

"Yes I did," I tell her. "Twice. She remembers it all."

"Your mother was wonderful to me," she says. "I've been such a vain brat, all my life. And all that time I didn't know she was plain. I really didn't. When you look at her you don't see a face, you see someone who loves you, no matter what."

Her grip becomes a little tighter, is, I think, as tight as she can make it. She leaves me to go back to fighting the pain.

I realize I have not been asked to bring my mother's forgiveness here. Or have I? Is my mother counting on me to pass it on or to live with it? I don't want her compromised. I don't want her apologizing for an attitude she was entitled to. But she has recanted, to herself, to the air in her hospital room, to me. I have to say the words here, in this room, whether or not I want to.

"She said you gave pleasure the way a sunset does, or a lace tablecloth."

For an instant the tension on my aunt's face relaxes and I want her to sit up and hold me. I think how proud I will be if this face reappears to me in a grandchild. I must carry the gene, somewhere; I hope I have passed it on unharmed.

I hear someone come into the room. Jo-Anne moves around the bed to the other side and she is lovely. I slip my hand out from under my aunt's to make room for hers. My aunt opens her eyes at the movement of hands and sees us both.

"Tell your mother that I think we've done a bang-up job, both of us. Tell her I'll see her in the line-up for rewards." This is not the mockery it would have been another time.

I kiss her lightly on the cheek. My lips leave a faint red print so I take a tissue from the box on her night table, sure she will not want to be left smudged. "Don't touch that," she says.

In a matter of days these two women will be gone; I can already see the world without them. Beyond my cousin's head, the red sun is fully risen now, a gaudy disrespectful whore of a sun, shining down on children in their beds, warming them.

I can feel in the palms of my hands what passed from sister to sister when they posed for the picture on that shared summer day. It is not unlike the grace I have carried from one to the other this dismal winter morning. And still there is no comfort. There is only the sun, and the steady wet snow.

Good women, full of grace. Stay with me.

The Appointment

The cab driver has beautiful teeth. He also has long dark hair and a frizzy beard, as so many of them do. His fingers are filthy, his sweater matted and his beard full of crud. But he only pretends not to care about himself. When he's alone in his bathroom, he takes care of his teeth. Sarah imagines a capable mother somewhere who taught him about his teeth when he was small.

He wasn't long getting to her house but even so the wind is bad enough out there this morning that she was anxious to climb into the warmth of the cab. She gives him the address of the dental building and he starts in on her. Bang.

"And how is madam this morning?" Sarcastic. Mean. She doesn't see how she deserves it. Maybe she should have got into the back seat. She has material status, enough for the back seat arrogance exercised by some of her peers, but she doesn't use it much. Maybe it wouldn't have made any difference. As they move down the elm-lined street, his hands fly around him, to the radio, to the gearshift, to his beard, gesturing toward her, stirring up the odour of dried perspiration.

She tries. She says, "You're American?", knowing full well he is, recognizing the accent from miles of Kennedy footage.

"Bet your ass, sweetheart," he answers. "One of Uncle Sam's finest. Raised on milk and red meat." He bares his teeth at her and she thinks of him tearing at raw beef. She is sure he has never been served raw beef; his mother carefully prepared and cut his meat for him until he was old enough to do it himself. Just as she does. She asks him if he saw the football game on Sunday and wraps her hand around the door handle.

"Hey ma'am," he says. "You know what gooks are?"

She turns her head away from him and watches the traffic. They are at the bridge and he is weaving in and out, tailgating innocent cars.

"Gooks are slime," he says. "Gooks grow in trees. You're looking at a gook killer, ma'am. Offed eleven, all by my lonesome. All sizes. I wanted a dozen but they wouldn't let me loose. They said I was over-excited." He throws his head back and barks his laugh at the roof of the cab.

Sarah has imagined killing. The usual thing: if ever she found herself alone, attacked; if anyone hurt any of the kids, deliberately. She has never imagined making a game of it. There is no getting out now, the traffic around them is thick and fast.

"You think you know what hot is, lady? You think you know what wet is? You know sweet shit all. That is precisely what you and everybody else knows. Sweet shit all. I've had the pleasure of running from a buddy just as he croaked. Bet you haven't."

He sits up straight and mimics a formal voice. "Many of my friends are going back. They feel fine now. Oh my, yes. They're just gonna suck right back to their big tit of a country and everything's gonna be sweet. Me, I'm staying here in this God-forsaken frozen slab you call home."

She says she is sorry.

"Sweet Jesus," he says. "You're sorry."

She could take the stance of mother, give him that kind of caring. It would be easy enough. Or she could dredge up some feminine, womanly phrase, subtle, but warm and soothing, give him his value as a male, distract him. She certainly doesn't feel responsible for his condition; nobody called from Washington to ask her if she thought war was a good idea.

She does the most awkward, worst possible, thing. When they finally stop she gives him a twenty dollar bill and climbs out before he can give her change, though he searches around in his pockets. She can hear his sneering, "Shit," and again, "You know sweet shit all," as she turns to close the door and says thank you. She doesn't feel conned. She wants to say why don't you buy a bottle to share with a friend from the cab company, and then she can't believe she wants to say something so ridiculous. Then she thinks maybe she should have said it.

The pain-killer she took before breakfast is wearing off; she can feel the rot in her molar. She reminds herself to make appointments for the kids on her way out. It shouldn't be long. There's only one person ahead of her and he's young, she doubts he's having root canal work. The chairs have been redone in taupe since her last appointment. Everything in this city is taupe. Or grey. Frank Sinatra is singing "My Way" and the pain comes in beats as well, blood beats. She wishes she could get a look at the tooth, inside, where the poison is festering at the nerve. She wishes she could clean it out, or air it. Jack told her to plan on an hour in his chair; he thinks there's a chance the thing can be saved.

She knows about war. She sees herself at fifteen, in front of a dark casket, after school. Her boyfriend stands in a suit at the head of the casket, shaking hands with neighbours and friends, watching his mother. His father had had a quick cancer, she can't remember which one, but his story was a war story. He'd been found in the North Atlantic, in a lifeboat, the only one alive. Seven others dead with him. She didn't ever know why the ship went down, just that it did and that he was days in the lifeboat, watching men die, likely trying to help. But what would you do? There wouldn't even be a dry coat to throw over someone. British surgeons had amputated an arm and a foot to keep him alive and that's how he came home. That was his story. She knew him as a friendly teasing father with a dark moustache, very European. At lunch on Sundays after church he would threaten to make her blush and then save her from it.

Two of her uncles had gone to war. They'd signed up brashly, that's what her grandmother said, telling the third brother that he too was essential, on the farm. That was their initial, innocent bravery. One came home with pale surgical scars, which her mother seemed to know all about, and a forced smile. One was left behind, in France, buried with his comrades-in-arms. Whenever she saw films of those fields, and she saw plenty, she chose one of the crosses and named it her uncle's, watching it while the camera panned away to other crosses.

The dead brother had been her mother's favourite; he was remembered as kind and full of the devil. These traits were watched for in her own generation and when they appeared, he was credited. She grew up with his sons. There'd been a time when she was jealous of the concern and attention given them but of course they'd had no choice but to take it and thrive under it. No-one asked them if they would have preferred to have a live father, like hers. In the midst of brooches and church programs and ropes of pearls on her mother's dresser, there was always a picture of a very young soldier with a hearty smile.

People carried on. It was a big price but it had to be paid. Things got better. The evil fascist was dead in his bunker and it would never happen again.

It's her turn. Jack's young assistant stands in front of her calling her by name. She gets up, running her tongue along the ridges of her teeth, counting what will be left if the root canal doesn't work.

Jack, who is middle-aged and fit and smiling, welcomes her to his chair. He presses the buttons on his console and she is prone, opening her mouth. He probes around, all the while talking about the Raffi concert they'd both attended, asking about her husband and the kids. He slips the long needle into her gums, several times, then leaves to check on another patient. She waits while the pain diminishes. She's not averse to needles; she's never had one that didn't help and who can resist the easing of pain? She closes her eyes.

She remembers the clipping she cut from the newspaper, years ago: two remembrance notices, one under the other. She hadn't taken it because it referred to war particularly but because of the odd balance it represented. She still has it, she's sure, in the drawer where she keeps all her strange mementoes. Both write-ups are about an inch long. Both sons died in France on February 19th, 1944. One had a familiar, easily pronounced name, like hers; one had a German name. She wondered for a second when she was cutting if they'd killed each other and then realized that was hardly likely.

Jack is back with his drill. He explains the process but she's not interested. He'll do what he can to save the tooth; he's very good. If he can't, he'll fit her with something false to chew with and she'll be content. The cavity isn't his responsibility. He's only helping. She wants to ask him if he and his family still honour Remembrance Day, if he has taught his children about the war. She wonders if he has an uncle buried in France with hers. All those crosses have to be somebody's uncles. But this is not the time for conversation. He's blasting away at the old filling and he won't want to stop to talk about war.

He's not hurting her and if she doesn't think about what he's doing and what he's going to find under that filling, she'll be all right. She always dreams when she is in his chair, a trick which makes her a good patient. She's tried to teach this trick to the kids but they will have none of it. They always want to know exactly what's going on. They ask Jack what he's doing and what it looks like and can they have a mirror to see the hole or the blood. If he hurts them, which is rare, they yell. She opens her eyes to see his face, intent on his work. She closes them again.

She remembers all the ordinary town men, the one who owned the restaurant, the one who sold Chevrolets, the undertaker-furniture dealer, dressed suddenly each November 11th in their grey pants and navy blazers and berets. She remembers the dank smell of them and their slow strides as they marched down the front street to the cenotaph, always in the cold rain, just like in the movies. There was a bronze plaque with about a dozen names chiselled into it attached to the front of the grey pillar. The man who made the gravestones must have made that pillar, because that's what it was, a gravestone, erected over empty soil. He'd made it large and forceful, confident against the dismal sky. To signify the win. Neither her gang nor any other had ever defaced it, though they etched their names and maxims on brick walls and telephone poles and the windows of crotchety old men, all over town. She'd thought when she was young that they'd respected it but she knows now what they felt was fear; not the complicated fear they took with them to the graveyard, but a simpler fear.

Jack is pushing cotton into her tooth, sopping up whatever he has found. He smiles down at her and puts his hand briefly on her shoulder, telling her that it won't be long, that the nerve will come out easily now. Maybe tonight at supper she'll say, I've lost my nerve, and her husband will groan and laugh.

She knows at least one more thing about war. She knows about Tom, her college room-mate's American boyfriend. They spent their summers at the beach if they could and the border was only a few miles way. The friendship and lust of Americans was unavoidable. Not that they'd tried to avoid it. They met Tom at the beach in early June and he stayed around for the summer, shadowing her room-mate and working illegally at the drive-in, flipping hamburgers. When he was drafted that fall he came back up for a quick last visit. There weren't any stories then, not that she'd heard anyway, and certainly no technically beautiful movies featuring Russian roulette and corpses, though she'd see all the movies later. The three of them sat together drinking coffee, knowing the thing was far away and likely very hot and dangerous, it was war after all. But none of them knew the particulars. They talked about the beach and about a guy she'd gone out with who didn't stay around for the summer and about another friend who had convinced the draft board that he was gay, though Tom was sure he wasn't, and how awful that was because he'd actually slept with some guys and would likely continue, according to Tom, because they'd be watching him. They talked about their courses and suddenly, with no warning to herself or to them, she began to cry. She sobbed like a fool and they asked her what was wrong and she could only say, you mustn't go. Her room-mate, laughing, tried to settle her down, saying it's me who should be crying, not you. She laughed with them and did her best to calm herself. When she couldn't they went out for pizza without her.

Tom came back a couple of years later and he had changed, of course. There was a shiftiness in his eyes where hell-bent nerve had been. Her room-mate said he didn't like to be touched. He wouldn't look at Sarah or talk, though she still has a gold chain he gave her. His father had died while he was gone and he had lots of money, which he spent on everyone. Then he roared off back to Detroit in his Corvette.

Jack is nudging her, smiling his straight white smile, saying he just has to treat the area with a special solution, which won't taste very good, and then he's going to give her a temporary filling. Her mouth feels leaden and huge. While she has the chance, she dips her tongue into the soft cavern where the nerve used to be. He is telling her that it will drain and heal and then he will fill it permanently and that she should be all right with it for years, maybe forever.

His assistant has mixed the filling and he is pressing it down, bit by bit, into the tooth. She locks her jaw and holds her head firm, giving him something to push against. She thinks about the wars being fought as she sits in this chair, the ones whose freshly dead soldiers she sees on "The National" every night. She thinks about the wars she studied as a girl: the Battle of Hastings, 1066; Waterloo; the Boer War; the Crusades. And more: the War of the Roses; the War of Independence; the Mesopotamian Wars; the Great War; the war she learned about in Sunday school, between God and the archangel.

She clears her throat and tells Jack that she has to make appointments for the kids. She wants to ask him if he thinks it would be wise to move closer to the uranium mines. She wants to ask him if he thinks the lucky ones will be vapourized in seconds, as that woman from New Zealand promises.

The Knife Sharpener

"Now tell me again," Janet said, wrapping the yellow scarf around her daughter's neck. Erin was dark, like her mother, with unruly curly hair framing an open face. She began her singsong.

"Don't dawdle, don't play with the dogs, don't talk to anyone I don't know. Go right to Kathleen's house." Kathleen was the twelve-year-old daughter of a friend and she had agreed to walk Erin to school the first year.

"Right," Janet opened the back door. "Off you go. See you at lunch." Mitsy ran up with Daniel in tow.

"Kiss and hug," she demanded. "Kiss and hug for me."

Daniel threw himself into the huddle, his arms raised and eager. After a minute Janet broke them up. "Okay, okay, enough." She herded the little ones back into the den. "Play," she said.

Erin stood hanging on the doorknob, waiting for her mother's hug. She accepted it like a talisman, safer after. "Love you Mom. Bye." She hurried down the steps.

Janet closed the door. She walked back up through the kitchen, grabbed her cigarettes and went to the living room window. From there she could watch Erin march down the driveway and across the street, making her way to the corner, where she turned out of sight. The neighbour, the older woman whose children were grown, sometimes watched Erin too. She'd told Janet that the child walked just like her mother. It was a kind of hurried saunter, a shuffle, anything but graceful. Janet lit her cigarette. Here and there, patches of the road had been worn by traffic to blue-black ice. The smaller kids on the street ran to those patches, sliding as fast and as far as they could, but always later in the morning, when the neighbourhood traffic had ceased and the street was quiet. For the past few years Janet and the other mothers had taken informal turns supervising the play and even when she was not on patrol, pacing and jumping in her parka and mukluks, she watched from the living room window. This year Erin would not be involved in the games. She was off, on her own.

Mitsy and Daniel stood with Janet now, their hands pressed against the cold window. Mitsy wrapped her arms around her mother's leg. "Time for toast," she said.

Daniel joined in, happy to hear a word he could echo. "Toast," he said. "Toast, toast, toast and jam."

"Okay." Janet took a hand in each of her own. "Let's do it."

The kids hauled themselves up to their places at the table while Janet dropped some bread into the toaster and eased the handle down to catch. She got the peanut butter and jam out and cleared Erin's cereal and juice away. The kids sat quietly, eyeing each other. Any minute some squabble would break out and then in another minute they would be best friends again. It would go on like that all day. She wondered when real long-lasting malice would begin. She'd seen hints of it in Erin, big hints.

The toast popped up.

"There it is," Daniel yelled.

She made herself a cup of coffee and sat down with them. Erin will be in school by now, she thought, will be taking off her coat and scarf and boots and sitting down at her desk, ready.

When the kids had finished eating she took them to the TV in the den. They settled down in front of "Romper Room", waiting for their instructions from the young woman who would lead them through their romps. Janet looked at the woman's perfect face. "You do a fine job," she said. "You're a good broad."

She spoke to the backs on the floor. "I'm going up to shower now. I'll leave the bathroom door open." They ignored her.

She hurried upstairs and made the beds. One of her husband's jackets hung on the bedroom door. That meant it needed a button; the button would be in the pocket. She stripped in the hall, tossing her nightie down the chute before going to the bathroom to turn on the water. Then back to the top of the stairs to listen for any noise other than the voice of Miss whatever-her-name-was on TV. Then into the shower. She sudsed her hair and groaned into the steamy water. Someday she would stand there for an hour, just stand, steaming, wasting water.

Afterwards, downstairs to check the kids and downstairs again to the wash in the basement. Left, right, white, coloured; left, right, white, coloured. She threw the white into the washer. Then upstairs to the bananas. They were past eating raw, ready to be made into muffins. She'd do this, check the mail, have another coffee. Then the kids. Hold them. Tell them there would be muffins.

She was mashing the bananas when the back doorbell rang. Oh go away, she thought, leave me be. But she went to the door and opened it. It was an old man.

"Yes?" she said.

"Morning." He tipped an imaginary hat to her. "I was wondering if you'd have any knives that could use sharpening?"

He was tall but his shoulders were stooped under the sloppy sleeves of a heavy grey curling sweater. It was not zippered and she could see suspenders. They held up dingy brown draped pants, the kind the young guys were wearing again now, but these were from some former life in the world of fashion. A satchel hung over his shoulder, bulky with something heavy. His face, fleshier than the rest of him, was a sickly, ashen colour. Her eyes finally settled on his. They were clear and alert, under bushy grey eyebrows. Well, he's not a drunk, she thought.

"Knives?" she asked.

"Maybe you've heard from your neighbours. I come round every March. Do mowers as well." He bundled his sweater around his chest, moving his weight from one foot to the other.

"Come in," Janet said. "You're cold." She closed the door behind him. "I guess I likely have some that aren't as sharp as they might be. How much do you charge?"

"That's up to you, Mrs.," he said.

Janet started toward the kitchen. "Come this way. I'll give you the knives. The mower's in the basement."

Mitsy and Daniel erupted from their play trance. "Hi," Mitsy said. "Who are you?"

Janet shooed them away from the knife sharpener. She led him to the kitchen drawer and handed him the knives, one after another. "These, I guess."

Downstairs in the basement, she pointed to her husband's workshop. "The mower's in there. I'll leave you to it."

She watched him look around. He dragged a lawn chair over to the workbench, opened his satchel and took out his whetstone.

Janet went to the washer, emptied the white load into the dryer, threw in the coloured and left him to go upstairs. The kids were busy with Lego. She finished the muffins.

Then Mitsy was at her knees.

"Hi, sweetheart," she said. "I'm coming to sit with you." She led her by the hand down into the den. They sat on the floor with Daniel and he pointed to the abstraction he'd built. "Tree," he said.

She played with them, letting them roll over and around her like bear cubs. Between squeals, she could hear from the basement the rhythmic scrape of steel against whetstone. She wondered if he could hear the squeals. The timer buzzed.

"Muffins!" she said.

The kids ran ahead of her, stopping just short of the stove. She pushed them back so she could open the oven door. "They have to cool a bit." She dumped the pans upside-down on the counter. Steam rushed up to her face and a sweet banana smell filled the kitchen. The kids danced around her. "In a minute," she said.

She put the kettle on for tea. He can likely smell the muffins, she thought. She reached for the cups and got the tray out from behind the spices. Two hands reached up over the counter and she put a steaming muffin in each. "Blow on them," she warned. "I'm going downstairs. You eat your muffins with Big Bird." They wandered off, watching their muffins as they carried them.

When the tea was ready, she arranged the pot and cups on the tray with a plate of muffins and carried it down to him. He was bent over his work, his knees braced under his thickly muscled arms. He didn't see her until she was right in front of him. He jumped a little.

"Thought you might like some tea and muffins." She put the tray on the workbench.

"Don't mind if I do," he said. He set the knife he was working on down beside him on the floor, the whetstone on his lap. "This is one fine old house," he said. "Tell by the shape of the basement." He waited for her to pour his tea.

"Yes," she said. "It's got some creaks and cracks but we like it." She leaned against the wall.

He took a muffin. "What line of work's your husband in?" he asked.

"He's an architect," she answered.

"That'd be interesting," he nodded.

"Are you retired from something?" Janet asked. "I'm guessing this is sort of a hobby?"

He leaned back to give her room as she poured his tea. "Retired from a lot of things," he chuckled. "Never been very lucky with a career." He took a sip of tea and added some milk. "Had jobs, though. Some good, some not so good."

Janet thought about her father. He'd been lucky; he'd made it. All the men in her life had made it, one way or another.

"I quit regular work when my wife died," he said. "She need-ed money more than I ever did."

"I'm sorry," Janet offered.

"Oh, that's all right," he said. "We didn't get along anyway. She spent most of her time hanging over a Bingo card, anxious for the big win. Did make a good pot of tea, though. Like you. I miss a woman pouring my tea.''

"You have children?'' Janet asked.

"Two,'' he said. "The young lady took off with the scum of the earth when she was sixteen and my boy's over in the North Sea, drilling for oil. He don't write much but I follow the papers to see what's going on over there. His mother used to worry over him but I don't. He's a hell of a swimmer. If the thing threatened to blow, he'd be the first one off, guaranteed.'' He broke a muffin open and wiped his mouth with the sleeve of his sweater.

Janet saw that the cuff was unravelling, eating away at itself. "That would be a good high-paying job for a young man,'' she said.

"He's not so young,'' he said. "He came home two years ago to bury his mother and he was thirty-five then.''

Janet was sorry she'd poured a cup for herself and she finished it quickly.

He put his teacup on the tray. "Thanks a million,'' he said. He picked up his whetstone. "I better get to work here.''

"And I better get back upstairs,'' Janet said. "My oldest will be home soon. I'll leave the muffins for you.''

"How old's she?'' the knife sharpener asked.

"Six,'' Janet answered.

"That's a nice age,'' he said.

She left him to finish, got the clothes out of the dryer and put the coloured load in. Upstairs, she dumped the clothes on the floor with the kids and began to fold. The back door flew open.

Erin ran across the rug and threw herself into the mess of clothes and arms on the floor. "I'm home,'' she said.

"Boots off,'' Janet said. "How was school this morning?''

Erin trudged back to the door, kicking off her boots. "We did art,'' she said. "Real art.''

The kids looked at something behind Janet. It was the knife sharpener.

"Finished,'' he said.

"Oh, good,'' Janet got up from the floor. "I'll get my purse.''

Erin came back into the room. "You're not the plumber,'' she said.

"No,'' he answered. "I just had tea with your mommy and sharpened some things for her.''

Janet stood beside him, offering a ten dollar bill. "Is this all right?''

"That's good, Mrs. Thank you.''

Erin had come to stand in front of her mother, wrapping Janet's arms around her chest.

"I was wondering if you'd like to stay and have lunch with us?" Janet asked. "Just soup."

"No," he said. "I'll be off, thank you." He walked over to the door, turning to wave at the kids as he let himself out.

They all admired Erin's school work, her bold triangles and shaky circles, then Janet went up to put the soup on to heat. She saw the knives on the counter. She was glad she'd had them sharpened. They were overdue. She gathered them up in a bunch and put them into an upper cupboard. They'd have to stay there for a while; the kids wouldn't know how sharp they were until one of them was cut and bleeding.

After lunch, Janet stood at the living room window again, watching Erin, admiring the way she swung her book bag. As the child crossed the street, she took a good run at a sheet of ice, skidding across it and tripping up onto the sidewalk. Erin, the name book said: a fair jewel set in a tranquil sea. Janet wondered if hard work and luck would bring her a good old age with her children. She wondered about the places downtown that offered some warmth, some company. Old hotels, there were six or seven of them, close to the Bay.

She saw him clearly, standing at the corner, his hand outstretched to Erin. Erin gave a little skip then took his hand; Janet had seen her take her grandfather's hand just that way. They walked together around the corner.

She ran back to Mitsy and Daniel in the den. They were watching "Mister Rogers". "Don't move," she said. "I just have to go out for a minute."

She grabbed her coat from the closet and was out the door and half-way down the driveway before she had it on. She ran as hard as she could, down to the corner and around it. Nothing. They were gone. There were two lanes mid-way down the block, one going south, one north, back toward the house. Don't call her name, she told herself. Don't call her name. There are garages, empty yards, shrubs to hide in. She decided on the lane going south. That's where he'd take her. She ran across the street. Her slippers were slapping hard on the icy pavement, loud. She kicked them off and started down the lane in her stockinged feet. She looked in the yards on each side as she ran, looked in every filthy garage window, in every overgrown space between house and fence.

She saw Erin's scarf snagged around the stuccoed corner of a garage twenty yards ahead. She let loose, let everything she had go to her legs.

She found Erin tucked into an evergreen hedge. The knife sharpener was crouched down talking to her in a gentle old man's voice. Janet pulled her away from him, turning the small face into the front of her coat.

The knife sharpener stood up and started to back away from them. "I wouldn't have hurt her, Mrs."

"Just what the hell would you have done with her then? Just what the hell do you think . . ." Janet heard the ugly edge to her voice and she knew she'd have to stop. Erin had taken her hand.

The knife sharpener was edging back, along the wall of the garage. "Please don't call the police," he said.

"What choice do I have?" Janet asked. She saw Erin watching, listening.

They turned their backs on him, walking down the lane and out into the street. She found her slippers there, overturned in the snow and she put them on. Erin hadn't said anything. Just keep quiet, Janet told herself, let her questions sort themselves out. She'll ask the right one. They were nearly at Kathleen's house.

"I shouldn't have gone with him, should I?" Erin looked down at her boots. "He was a stranger."

"No," Janet said. "You shouldn't have. You can know strangers a little bit but they're still strangers."

Erin kicked at the snow. "I thought he was a friend of yours."

Kathleen ran noisily toward them. "Where've you been?" she asked. "My mom's been phoning. We're late. C'mon."

"Hi," Erin said calmly, as though nothing had happened to her. She took her friend's hand. "See you later, Mom."

"Wait, Kathleen," Janet put her hand on the girl's book bag. "You be sure you don't talk to anyone you don't know. All right?"

"I never do. What's wrong?" she asked.

"Just make sure, that's all. I'll talk to your mom this afternoon." Janet watched the two of them go off down the street. Erin was leaning, just slightly, into Kathleen's shoulder. She turned back toward the house and, remembering Mitsy and Daniel, began to run again.

They were fine. They had all the muffins, some half eaten, spread out around them on the floor. "Mister Rogers" was still on. Janet looked at the screen, at his kind face, at his kind cardigan sweater. She felt her feet stinging from the cold.

She went to the living room window with her cigarettes. The snow on the lawns was blue-white in the sun and the black ice on the street had been covered with a light dusting of snow she hadn't seen fall.

She had choices. She could call her husband, who would likely call the police. She could describe the knife sharpener. She could make it so bad for him that he'd never show his face in their world again. Or she could say absolutely nothing, to anyone, ever.

She could take a calm liberal stance. She could get in the Toyota and find him, talk to him, listen to him. She could remind him of his own daughter, when she was small and trusting on his knee. Before she took off with the scum of the earth.

Or she could take the grey ceramic ashtray from the coffee table and hurl it across the room at the fireplace where it would shatter and come to rest in pieces among the ashes.

The Model

She is long-legged, as you would expect her to be, and tall and tireless. Her high cheekbones suggest the beauty of other races, other epochs, richer than this one. The rhythm of her own very special stride begins to release itself in her pelvis as she waits behind the partition which separates the dressing room from the ramp. Beyond the partition, the red-carpeted ramp forms a T-shape out into the darkened crowd of women, small lights edging it, erupting one after the other like a marquee.

The sumptuous touch of fine cloth on her flawless skin and the music, which is only the primitive thump of bass dressed up in frilly strings and hard brass, calm her down to the bone. As soon as the Chinese silk is off, she moves.

The other models on the ramp, elegant and unrestrained, catch the music's rhythm with their hips and turns and flashes of flesh, giving their pure white smiles generously to the black air above the crowd. The ramp heaves with their movement.

The black mink swings loose and full around her body. She wore chinchilla last week, in another city, and she remembers the weight of it swinging back in against her as she turned. At the intersection she unwraps, throwing the coat down, dragging it behind her like a cave woman with a hide. The cherry-red swim suit brings the crowd to silence; not many watching would be able to imagine themselves in this one. The commentator does her number; "Get Away From It All", away from the mink, away to the sun.

She ducks around the corner of the partition, backstage again. She tosses the mink to one of the assistants and is out of the swim suit and half into the red taffeta Lady Diana imitation when the first cramp erupts behind the wall of her hard, flat abdomen. She thinks it's her period, the rough beginning. She has long ago given up trying to be ready for it.

She's tried pills, has asked her gynecologist for the special mix that muffles all the estrogen and stops the flow entirely but she'd been sick as a dog, bleary-eyed and dizzy and the doctor cut her off. He told her she'd have to live with the pain, as others did, and wrote out a prescription to ease it. The pills made her hungry and the hunger made her too fat by five pounds; the doctor offered other pills, with more of this and less of that. She asked then if he could just book her in and clean out whàt she'd never use anyway but he shook his head. He implanted a small plastic loop, forcing it carefully up into the soft tissue of her interior. He washed his hands and said it was the best he could do. And the pain had been lessened, until now, and she did trust the bit of plastic to intercede if any cocky little embryo thought to attach itself to her wall.

She'd lugged dolls around with her when she was a small dark-eyed girl, and she dressed them each once or twice in the perfectly lifelike outfits her grandmother had made for them. But there was boredom in her face and in her movements. Her parents noticed. They offered a miniature set of delicate blue china and a little table with a lace cloth and four Queen Anne chairs. She set it all up in her room, placed four of her dolls in the chairs around the table, and walked back to the curved staircase, sitting down on the top step with her dark braids pressed against the wall. Her parents offered a shelf in their library, emptied of Dickens and Dickinson and stocked with escape suited to her age and nature. She took three especially lively books upstairs and left them open on the pudgy laps of her dolls who were not at table. She was offered tuition in ballet. The ballet mistress, old and elegant with fragility, announced that the girl had a lovely sense of self. The deal was struck.

At Christmas she awoke to a white-framed mirror placed beside her window. It was adorned with tinsel and an oversized red bow, and tilted to receive her image as she emerged from the yellow down comforter. She felt blessed. At her adolescence, a new, larger mirror replaced the white one. It was held in a magnificent mahogany frame and had wings which she could adjust to multiply her image. Doubly, triply blessed. In the end her muscular discipline was not enough for the ballet mistress and she was excused from the lessons.

Young escorts arrived with corsages for her wrist and to a man they wiped their palms on their trousers before touching her bare, scented back. The cleaning lady maintained the dolls for years, dusted and arranged them on the window sills to suit herself.

She moves in place behind the partition, zipped and snapped and ready for her entrance in the red taffeta. This is the first gown in the show and as she advances along the ramp she can feel the sighs. This one will sell; someone out there has already decided, that gown is mine, I don't care what it costs.

She thinks about the reception which will follow the show. She will be expected to wear one of the designs; maybe it should be this one. She hates the receptions and is excused from them after the big shows, the ones for the buyers, but this is a public fund raiser. The women who have paid the hefty ticket price will want a chance to get close to the models, to stand beside them, sipping Dubonnet, measuring the length of their own legs, the width of their own hips, against perfection. Usually the women are old enough to have worked their stomachs down but those with money to stock their closets with clothes from shows like this never have it all, not any more. The breasts are always gone and usually the thighs. Calves hold, calves and stomachs and good faces. They'd buy the clothes that demand calves and stomachs, most of them, the smart ones.

Sometimes their babies tag along behind them at the receptions, svelte long-legged seventeen-year-olds who carry one of Daddy's charge cards in their leather bags. The red suit was for them. Sometimes the daddies come too and oh, don't they wish, and occasionally they get, days later, in the next city. They treat her like a red Porsche; aesthetically. Sometimes she grabs one of the boys who drive her from city to city. They are eager and unburdened.

She is at the farthest extension of the ramp when she cramps again, this time harder. She doesn't have time to stop her shoulders from hunching down toward the pain. She moves back to the partition and is behind it with the gown unzipped and the red pumps kicked away before the cramp subsides. She strips to her teddy and runs to the bathroom, locking the door behind her. There is no blood, not a drop. She rams a tissue between her flesh and the silk and runs back to the next gown. It is black velvet and strapless, held away at the front with heavy wires. She steps into it and then into the black sandals. Someone fastens a chunky bracelet on her wrist and she glances at the diamonds. It is not unusual for a local jeweller to add a touch of glamour.

This is the second most important gown in the show. She's had her hair done up in a tight top-knot just for this one. On the ramp, her hips make the velvet move, make it gather the lights and throw them off again and there is nothing, not the slightest movement of hair nor the release of one facial muscle to distract.

She nearly pulls it off. She is only five strides from the partition, has sold the black velvet to someone out there in the pit, when the big one hits. She can't stop her hands from going to her stomach this time and she pauses, ignoring the music for a few seconds while she concentrates on the pain. As soon as she can she walks past the startled commentator and forces her way through the half-dressed bodies to the bathroom. She can feel the lump moving down through her. She locks the bathroom door.

She glances at the cold white porcelain then turns and hikes the gown up to her hips and sits, waiting for the lump to drop, thinking about the plastic as it moves. She knows pushing would help but she doesn't know where the muscles are so she waits and the push comes on its own. She hears an odd plop in the water and takes some tissue to clean herself. Her fingers touch gristle and she looks. The plastic loop, beige and innocent, bobs at the edge of the pink water. The umbilical cord, transparent but for the thin red vein, is still attached to the bloody round thing sinking into the dark tunnel and it is still attached to her. She forces her hand to grip and pull. It isn't difficult at all; the thing slips away from its moorings with just a couple of tugs, bringing with it a rush of brighter blood. She flushes the toilet quickly, praying for uneventful disappearance. She waits for the flow to stop, sitting, clear headed now, looking into the mirror on the wall across from the toilet. The blood, it seems, has all come from her face; her complexion has changed and the make-up doesn't hide the greenish hue. Nothing this ugly has ever happened to her. She feels like an animal. She checks the water under her and wipes again, flushes again, wipes again. It doesn't stop.

She feels clammy. She reaches around behind to unzip the dress. She gathers and pulls it up over her head and spreads it out on the filthy tile floor. She moves carefully down to it, lies on her back, motionless. She can feel the black velvet soaking up the blood.

In the midst of a new dizziness, she thinks about the people who might come to her. Perhaps someone will notice that the black velvet gown is not back on its hanger, protected under plastic, or the jeweller, wandering around backstage with an empty bracelet case, will stop someone and demand to know where the hell she is. Perhaps one of the women will ask for her at the reception, or someone, passing the bathroom door, will try it, as people do. Perhaps someone among all those people has a nose for blood.

Moon Watcher

Marg gripped the cottage hammer, a heavy old claw, and swung again at the locks. They were badly rusted and misshapen from the hammer blows of other seasons. Though winter was over, the shutters still held tight against the wind off the lake; they waited, pale green and chipped and slightly warped, for release. She braced her back on the thick trunk of the front maple, the one whose branches she liked to hear thumping on the screen porch roof. Any thief could have had the contents of the cottage, such as they were, with a well placed boot against the door; the locks were meant to protect against natural elements and, though rusted and bent, they did that, quite dependably.

Marg had counted the jobs before she started and she guessed it would take more than double the usual time to get settled. The things her husband normally did would consume a lot of figuring-out time because she'd never paid much attention to them. She counselled herself, half-seriously, to give this fact some weight when she was deciding, after the jobs were done, whether or not to continue to have a husband.

When the shutters were all opened and fastened back, she moved away to assess her work. The early evening breeze off the lake caught the stiff porch screens and the screens returned the push. She saluted the porch with the hammer. She walked around to the lean-to shed behind the cottage and exchanged the hammer for the axe, moving to the wood pile where she chose a chunk of wood. Last fall, when the driver dumped the wood on a newly seeded patch of grass, Alec had ranted with dismay, had worked late into the night sorting and stacking it on a gravelly spot near the pump in his precise, deliberate way. She could still hear his dismay and she could hear the echo of his clear hard choppings. She wondered which of her noises would come, unsought, to him.

The axe felt heavy in Marg's hand, pulled on her arm. She had always been attracted to loud work noises, but making them was something else. She wanted to excuse herself to anyone who might be within earshot.

She missed and cursed the first piece of wood more than a few times before she connected with it. The noise was less than she had anticipated, but more surprising was the simple joy she felt in actually splitting the thing. She lined up another chunk and swung again. She felt someone behind her just as the axe connected the second time.

"Could you use a hand?" Marg turned toward a tall lumpy man. He wore baggy jeans and a peach-coloured golf shirt. Black curly hair filled the gap at the neck of his shirt and a beard, more white than black, grew around a small, narrow mouth. His eyes were round and frank and friendly. He offered his hand. "Rob," he said. "Rob Carrigan."

"Hello." Marg wiped her hands on her rear end and offered one. "Marg MacPhail."

"We heard some activity over here. We're in the Kemp place." His small mouth opened into a smile. "Rebecca is just making a new pot of coffee." He nodded at the wood pile. "I could finish a few of these."

"Is Mr. Kemp dead then?" Mr. Kemp had been their neighbour since they'd bought the place, ten years before. Marg had looked forward to watching him skim the sand of the nearby public beach with his metal finder this summer. He said he did it to collect enough silver to buy the light beer he favoured but Marg knew the contraption for what it was: company, a replacement for a wife who had died while napping in the Kemp front porch three summers before. She'd thought maybe this summer she'd walk with Mr. Kemp, maybe get her own metal finder.

Rob Carrigan withdrew a little. "The real estate woman said he died last fall. His kids didn't want the bother of the cottage."

"Sorry. I just liked him a lot." Marg picked up the axe. "The wood's fine, thanks anyway. I'll do a few more. Maybe I could have that coffee in the morning?" She laughed. "If I can move." Rob nodded again and said that would be fine and that they had some liniment if she found she needed it. He left.

It had always been the tradition among the cottagers that friendship was kept to a minimum. Everyone depended on a summer of effortless privacy; that's what made the place so peaceful. Marg did not relish the idea of teaching this tradition to the new people. She thought about strategy as she swung, with less energy now, at the wood.

She carried the wood in small loads into the living room and dumped it beside the fireplace. She found some faded funny papers and built a fire around a bunched-up pile of them. This, at least, had always been her job, and she knew the idiosyncrasies of the fireplace well. When the wood had taken, she gave herself a sponge bath and changed into her new red polo pyjamas, stopping in the tiny galley kitchen to pour herself a light scotch, without ice. She sank into her corner of the old maroon couch that faced the fireplace, letting the fatigue move around inside her, feeling it settle finally in her shoulders. The scotch and the fire lifted the chill from her and from the room, and as she listened to the snapping wood she imagined she heard her husband's voice, from his corner of the couch. But he was in the city, maybe in their bed, maybe not. He had an option. Since last October he'd been welcome in another bed.

Marg looked at her watch. She gave herself ten minutes to think about Alec. She had refused to think at all during the first few weeks she had known, told herself she didn't know at all, then she thought about the two of them together for days and nights running and then she stopped. It had begun when the dead leaves covered the lawns, with his missing just a few nights beside her; then he stayed home for a while and then he was gone nine nights in a row and then, quietly, home again. It was a pattern she couldn't read. She expected every piece of mail to be for her, from his lawyer.

When the delicate first snow began to fall she'd told him she could use an explanation and he gave her one: the woman had come to him, at him, from nowhere. He hadn't been looking for anything particularly, had been happy sometimes, a lot of times. But everything had changed once she was there in front of him, and he thought he had a right to something. Marg was dumbfounded and weak from thinking and not thinking; she told him she understood, she agreed, he did have a right.

She didn't know if this decency was achieved by some perverse Christian love or by her stunned inability to jump in and play the game to win, but she depended on it for as long as she could. When grief and rage began to overtake the decency, she signed up with a psychiatrist. He suggested that perhaps she wasn't as decent as she was in the habit of believing and sure enough, it turned out she wasn't. Given a little air, a little nurturing, the grief and rage thrived. Alec sensed the thriving. One night in bed he touched her elbow, said he wouldn't be leaving her but he needed time. Marg told him he could have time and she called the lawyer her brother had been urging her to call. Together they got Alec out of the house.

Now that Alec wanted the winter to be forgiven, to be put in the past, Marg had to make a decision. His wanting to come back was only his decision. She needed to picture him the way he was before he'd had a right to something, but all she could summon was his sorry, sorry face and the self-loathing which he wore like a complexion. She should have brought a photograph with her, the one of him bare-chested on the boat, leaning against the windshield, half-asleep. He didn't know she'd taken that picture, and she'd kept it for herself, in her panty-hose drawer. Even in her worst state of rage she hadn't thought of ripping it in half.

It had been too long a winter. She felt disdain now for everyone involved, herself included. Often, alone in bed, she wished someone would come to her and slice her back open, lift her spinal cord away from her flesh like the backbone of a well cooked lake trout, and leave her free of nerve endings. Her doctor said nothing about her problem was unusual, that many people found themselves in the same situation, that patterns were recognizable. She'd told him to put it in his ear.

The erratic shadows in the room brought Marg's attention back to the fire. She checked her watch. Too much time had passed, again.

She poured herself another, lighter scotch and walked outside, switching the porch light on as she passed. The grass was already wet, and her sneakers were soon soaked, so when she came to the hip-high fieldstone wall that separated the grass from the beach she sat on it, outside the half-circle of light thrown by the porch bulb. The lake water lapped harmlessly against the sand. The sky, much farther away and dark as anything could ever be, was lit with stars and the full summer moon. Always the moon. A cloud she hadn't seen drifted across the face of it, but the cloud was inconsequential, moved in a haphazard, trivial way and was soon gone, made invisible again by the darkness. It hadn't changed the moon; the moon could withstand anything. She damned Alec for not being beside her on the wall. If he were with her he would have made the ice, and when she moved her glass around, as she was in the habit of doing, she would have had the comfort of the sound of the ice.

Perhaps because of the silence, Marg felt someone out there with her, not close, but close enough. She turned toward a dark shape in front of the Kemp cottage, twenty yards away.

"Couldn't ask for a better moon." Rob Carrigan leaned against a maple trunk, just outside his own half-circle of light.

"Very dependable, that moon," she answered.

"I watched you walk out and sit down," he said. "I'm going in now and I want you to watch me."

Marg made a quirky face to herself in the dark, but she watched him anyway. This man Rob wore red polo pyjamas, identical to hers though a good deal sloppier, with the same pretentious label on the ass. As he swung the screen door open he assumed a quick model's stance, and she laughed louder than she might have on such a quiet night.

Her sleep in the middle of the sagging mattress was nearly dreamless. In the morning, still in her pyjamas, she hauled the chaise longue from the porch to the grass, beat the dust and cobwebs from it and went inside to make herself a tray of cereal and instant coffee. She was just back and settled when the wife came bouncing over in a bikini. It was pea green with dozens of tiny orange fish, some whole, some in bits where the bathing suit ended and flesh began. She walked in strides rather than steps and extended her hand to Marg long before it was necessary. This was not a woman Marg wanted to know.

"Hi," she said. "I'm Rebecca. I've heard all about you."

Marg found herself putting the tray carefully on the grass and heaving herself up out of the chaise. She asked herself if she had brushed her teeth.

"Nice to meet you." They shook hands, as at a conference.

"I won't stay to talk now, just going in for a dip. Catch you later." And the woman strode away, leaping over the fieldstone wall rather than taking the decrepit wooden steps that led to the beach, as any self-respecting forty-year-old woman would have.

Yes, you likely will, Marg thought, as she lowered herself into the chaise and set the tray on her thighs again. She didn't watch the woman swim. She kept her head bent over her mug, sipping her coffee. Her Raisin Bran was half gone before she felt Rob Carrigan this time.

"Morning," he said.

"And to you," she answered.

He sat in Mr. Kemp's old chaise with his back to her, eating breakfast in his red polo pyjamas. "What kind of cereal are you eating over there?"

Marg decided she didn't want to count coincidences all summer. She scouted her mind for an unlikely cereal, just in case.

"Cream of wheat. How about you?"

"Too bad," he said. "Raisin Bran."

Marg eyed the flakes of bran in her spoon.

"Do you play this game with everyone?" she asked.

"No," he laughed. "Never happened before. I've always wanted a double. Thought maybe you were mine."

"You feel the need of one?"

"Yup." He put his cereal bowl on the grass beside him. "Would you show me your cereal if I walked over there now?"

"It's gone," Marg lied.

"How about that cup of coffee when Becky comes back up?"

"Thanks no. I'm on a kind of retreat. Sorry if that sounds rude and I'm sorry about the cream of wheat."

"Understood," he said, and he took on an aura of permanent silence, and Marg wanted to say thank you but she held back. When Becky returned from her swim, Marg heard him mumble something to her and saw Becky shrug her shoulders. She leaned back and closed her eyes to avoid the woman's coming glance.

Well, that much had been accomplished. After a respectable time she went into the cottage, changed into a T-shirt and cut-offs and drove over to the point to talk to Jack. Jack was the handyman, mechanic and willing false idiot for all the summer people. She asked him if he could come over to show her how to get the boat down from its suspended moorings in the boathouse; he told her sure and right now seems as good a time as any, and he followed her back to the cottage in his blue half-ton. After he showed Marg how to work the pulleys and cranks and the boat sat rocking in the water, he got the motor from the back porch and put it on. He said he'd better run the boat over to his shop and give it a good servicing. She suspected he just wanted to take the thing for a macho spin across the lake, but then she thought no, that's just what he wants me to think; he's working on his summer personality. He roared off to the point.

Marg changed into her bathing suit and returned to the chaise longue, turning it a bit, away from the Kemp cottage and into the sun. She'd found a mildewed homemaker's magazine in the cottage and she leafed through it. A still-bright lead page with bold yellow letters caught her eye. Cooking for one, it said. She read the first recipe. It was a small elegant dish, with obscure ingredients. She closed the book and opened her arms and legs to the sun. The yellow phrase reappeared in the darkness of each blank eye. She adapted the phrase. Paying the heat bill for one. Listening to jazz for one. Calling your seventy-year-old mother for one. Of course there would be friends, there damned well better be. Friends for one. Not so unnatural. She thought about the peripheral people, the ones who would have just enough interest in her to make small judgements over coffee. Alec liked to avoid divorced people, said divorced people tended to forget how to be private, assumed empathy when it wasn't necessarily there. Marg knew how wrong he was. Even just here, on the edge of divorce, she knew more about privacy than she had ever wanted to know, and nothing was assumed. Her thoughts wandered to some of Alec's other philosophies, and she didn't realize she'd fallen asleep until the homemaker's magazine slid from her belly and startled her awake. She had been dreaming. She knew she had because she could feel the edge of a sob caught in her throat. She looked over to the Kemp place, but no-one was there, not outside anyway. There could have been a movement from the porch to the inside of the cottage, but her eyes were dazed from the sun and she couldn't be sure.

The sound of the boat approaching and Jack's uncivilized yell took care of the dream. Marg walked, dizzy, over to the water. "Shipshape," Jack said. "Shipshape." He gave her the key. "You come in and settle up the next time you're over for groceries." She thanked him and walked him to his truck at the back of the cottage. As he was pulling away he leaned out the window. "Where's your old man?"

"Not here," she said.

"Well don't run her too hard the first few times out."

Marg leaned against the wood pile, watching him disappear around the bend in the road. After a time a grub tried to slip itself onto the back of her shoulder; she winced away and rubbed her skin hard. She went into the cottage to make some ice and — the pump, she remembered the pump. It should have been checked and flushed with Javex. She had used the water without thinking. Alec always muttered about mice when he worked on the pump at the beginning of the season. She'd have to go to the store for Javex if she wanted ice later.

She drove through the dust to the store. Jack's wife collected for his morning's work and Marg gathered up a few things she hadn't brought from home along with a bottle of bleach. Rob Carrigan leaned on her arm at the till.

"That for your pump or are you going to drink it?" His smile was not at all sure of itself or of Marg, and the peak of his Labatt's cap was at two o'clock.

"Pump," Marg said.

"Let me do it for you. Then I swear I'll never speak to you again." He grinned then; the grin was the kind that is good to see.

"Yes," Marg said.

He followed her back to the cottage, and each time she took a bend in the road Marg slowed until she could see him again in her rearview mirror. He drove steadily and sensibly, and she wondered if he knew his hat was on crooked.

He worked on the pump without a word. When he was finished and gone, Marg made two trays of ice cubes.

She leaned her head against the fridge, checked her watch. The trouble with the doctor was that he had no opinions. Every damned suggestion he made was countered with another, alternate one. She didn't need alternatives; she needed guidance. He said he wouldn't feel comfortable telling another human being what to do. "Who cares how you feel?" Marg had asked him. He answered this with his professional smile, and offered her more coffee.

It had been years since Marg had had a supercilious friend, not since university. She'd give something to have one now. She did have two fine ordinary friends who touched her more than was usual for them, and who made sure she had all the intimate lunches anyone could eat, but they, too, had no opinions. "Give it time," they said, separately. "Then you'll know."

She was almost used to missing Alec, the smell of him and his grunts and his sharp shoulders. Over the months she had assembled and arranged all the bits of him that came to her, like a patchwork quilt she could wrap around her shoulders when she felt chilled. The harder thing was the plain hurt. It was as if he had fouled the air that enclosed them, their own rich stale air, had opened some valve and allowed an unnatural odour to seep in when he should have kept that valve tight, as she did. Maybe if she'd tried harder to have kids; maybe if they'd adopted. Alec had wanted to. Kids might have helped.

Maybe if she flipped a coin. She could rest a coin on the ridge of her middle finger, flick it high and vow as she watched it sail up that she would live the rest of her life with the coin's decision and never look back, never. She could grab what she needed from the air, slap it against the back of her hand. It was preposterous to depend on time.

She'd known from the beginning that none of them could help her; her doctor, her friends, even Alec would have if it were possible.

But she couldn't do it alone, couldn't push hard enough to stop the balancing act she'd perfected. Something extra had to happen.

Marg's eyes moved to the window, an ordinary square of light and shade, and just in the instant before she would have looked away, Rob Carrigan placed himself exactly in the centre of what she saw. He was looking up at the branches of an old tree, dragging a wooden ladder under one arm and holding a red birdhouse in the other hand. He wore a carpenter's apron, bulky with hammer and nails, tied over his bathing suit.

She turned from him, to clear her head. She walked to the front of the cottage, down the beach to where the boat sat nudged against the sand by the water. She pushed it out into the lake and climbed over the side. The key was still on its hook in the cottage, the oars in the boathouse. She stayed there, thirty feet from shore, rocking. With her back to the shore she could see the point, dark and small and hazy, and that was all. There were no other boats on the water, just the end of the water at the horizon and a thin white line dividing one blue from the other. She turned to the cottages, saw how strange they were, how exposed in their clearing and how alike. The structure, the positioning, the idea of them, was identical; only paint and vines and a certain leaning here and there made them separate. The waves moved her to the shore. The answer would come tonight; she had no idea how but she knew there was no stopping it.

She went back into the cottage, to the fridge. The shrimp she'd brought from home had thawed, so she stir-fried it, adding onion and garlic and peppers and mushrooms. She stuck her nose into the steam. She'd cooked enough for two and she ate every bite of it. It had been a long time since she'd felt full-blown hunger; a long time since she'd felt satisfied. She cleaned up the dishes and drove over to the point to buy a book. It would have to be something good to get her though the next few hours. She almost wished she had brought some books with her, but then half the fun of the summers had always been letting Jack and his wife serve as literary guides. Their squeaky carousel offered Harlequins and obscure mysteries and lots of smut, and once in a while, at least a couple of times each summer, some colourful, renowned, paperback turned up that both she and Alec told themselves they'd been wanting to read for years. She chose a thin, dark blue book. On the cover, someone's idea of a heroine sat on a stump. Marg liked her hat.

Back in the cottage she changed into her pyjamas and started a fire in the fireplace. The ice was slushy hard; she dumped a tray into the sink, threw a couple of cubes into her glass and eased some scotch around them. She set the drink on the three-legged table beside her corner of the couch and settled into the book. She knew how things would go half-way into the first chapter, but she kept on, remembered what everyone looked like, what everyone said, offered far-fetched empathy to the far-fetched characters. Chapter by chapter, the time passed. She kept the fire high and hot.

When it was finally late enough she closed the book and tossed it on the cushion beside her. It slipped to the floor, and as she picked it up she noticed a moon behind the heroine, a fingernail moon, a quarter moon. She held the book tight in her hands. The moon did change, was diminished, was, now and then, according to the dictates of orbits and seasons, obliterated. She rubbed the moon with her thumb and she told herself it would be possible to give up her full strong moon out there over the water and believe finally in nothing much at all. It might make all the difference. She wouldn't have to feel any more than the moon feels. She could continue then, with Alec, wouldn't have to live through years of missing him, regretting things she couldn't even remember.

She put the book on the mantel, poured a second scotch and walked carefully out of the cottage, switching the porch light on as she passed. She walked through the light to the fieldstone wall and perched herself on it. She was shivering and thought about going back for a sweater, but no, everything should be the same. She felt him very close. He didn't speak.

"Have you got your pyjamas on?" she asked.

"Yup." She could hear him chuckling just over the sound of the small waves on the sand.

"I'm glad," she said.

"That's not what you want to ask me though, is it?"

Marg rattled the ice around in her glass. "What do you mean?"

"Just ask," he said.

She took off her runners and threw both legs over the fieldstone wall, easing herself down onto the sand. It was surprisingly cold. If she could have looked anywhere, deliberately, it would have been to him, but she didn't, she kept her eyes on her own cold bare feet in the cold bare sand, commanding him, with no sign, to follow her. He did. He came to walk with her.

They walked toward the boat and then around it and down the beach. He hiked his red pyjama legs up to his knees and waded, tentatively, into the lake water. Marg kept to the sand, and they had moved well down the beach when he offered his hand. He didn't move out of the water toward her; she was to come to him. She hiked up her own pyjama legs. Just as her hand went into his bigger, stronger hand, he kicked a footload of water at her, soaking her, chilling her immediately, startling her more than a slap on the face could have. He stood poised, ready to run. Marg looked at his face and she knew it could go either way, she had a choice; she could cry and wheel around, run back to the cottage where she could strip down and warm herself in front of the fire, or she could soak him. She wondered how fast she could move, that had to be part of the decision; she wanted a fair fight. She missed and half-fell on the first try, but on the second she got him, turned the bright red of his crotch dark. She took off back toward the cottage, running hard through the moonlit sand, and she nearly made it, nearly escaped, but he followed her, panting, finally catching the arm she had flung behind her in flight and whoosh, her rear was soaked. She laughed then, a loud rude eruption, and she scooped her arms down into the lake and soaked him again, hesitating before taking off, thinking it might be over, watching his face for the sign. He was bent over double with laughter, his hands on his knees, catching his breath in short hard puffs. He looked up to Marg for the sign.

The voice came to them from the fieldstone wall. It was Becky's. ''Fun?'' she wanted to know.

She stood with one of Rob's sweaters pulled over her nightgown, exposed by the light from the moon. Marg felt her cold wet arm go up in welcome, waving her down, inviting her to join them, as if what they were having was fun. Becky's head moved just enough to indicate refusal. Rob had stopped grinning, stood with his back to his wife, and Marg recognized on his face the hard old need she had been so long without. He's helping me, she thought. He's doing what he can. Then she saw Becky vault the fieldstone wall, land upright in the sand. She was pulling Rob's sweater up over her head; her nightgown was pale blue satin. Marg tried, in that split second of privacy, to acknowledge Rob's gift. A hug was out of the question, but there was time for a slight quickening of her lower lip and she watched his eyes to make sure he'd seen it. She wasn't convinced that she had faked the quickening or that it mattered if she had.

She turned her back on them then and stripped down to her goose-pimpled flesh, leaving her pyjamas in a heap on the sand. She lined herself up with the ancient path laid by the moon and ran through the water until it was high on her legs. She swam hard, visible to anyone who might be watching the iridescence on the face of the water.

Wolf Spiders

He decided it was the female resting dead centre in the web, though he hadn't seen her build it. She'd been there when he came out at six to wait for the sun. The web wasn't exotic, it was the kind a kid would draw if you asked him to draw a spider's web; it looped from one of the sunporch studs over to the rusted eavestrough. The strands looked thicker, tougher than expected. The only delicacy was in the outside edges.

Why is she white, he wondered. He thought he might go down to the basement later and dig out the kids' old encyclopedia, see if he couldn't find something on colouration, or the lack of it. Albino? A gene, or a chromosome, he couldn't argue which, gone wrong? He remembered the diagrams, DNA, RNA, the shaky X's, the broken tips. The chinks in the old master plan.

He saw her mate, equally pale, moving along the outside wall of the house, trying to hide among the coarse stones in the stucco. Maybe he was watching her, guarding her. Maybe he was watching him, inside the sunporch, through the screen. Maybe he was blind. Albinos were, often.

Maybe they were both blind, white and blind, just doing their thing, building their web and making love after a little wine, waiting for the blessed event. Eggs? he wondered, or born alive? He'd get a book, go over to the library if he had to. He was going to watch and he wanted to know beforehand, eggs, or born alive. He wondered which would be worse. And how many there might be. If they didn't come out in sunlight, he could wait with the flashlight, there was a good chance she wouldn't know the difference. And even if she did, even if she had sensors which could pick up his presence, he would still see, she wouldn't be able to stop herself. And she wouldn't want to leave the web.

She was big, her abdomen looked like an oversized chick pea, rounded. Her legs, eight of them, he'd counted, were as white as the rest of her; he could see their segments, clearly defined, and busy. As if she couldn't stop, though the work looked finished.

He took his eyes from her and went into the house to freshen his drink. It wasn't yet seven by the clock on the stove. He heard nothing from upstairs, nothing from his wife, nothing from their nearly grown offspring. He would tell them when they came down about his spiders, would ask them to come and watch with him, one at a time. At least the kids. They might be interested. And she might too. Depending. On how her dreams had left her, on what mood her first waking thought had found. He'd go back to the sunporch and concentrate on her first waking thought, send her a good one, a cheery one. That's what he'd do while he waited with his spiders. He returned to the sunporch and sat down with his drink, leaning forward over it.

Think sandy beach, he thought.

Think your aunt's emerald ring, which you lost so long ago in the park, pushing the kids on the swing, and found again, just outside the circle of dirt beat flat by stopping feet.

Think coming like a loud young beast in my arms.

Think old things.

The male had moved again. He was climbing onto the web, getting his bearings on the delicate outside strands. There, he was on. The web reverberated with his extra weight; she didn't flinch. Even if she was blind, she would know where he was, she would have in her mind a grid, a pattern, would be able to sense its emptiness, or fullness. She would know him by his weight, the way he moved, or didn't move. He would have a style, a particular spider style which she would know in her heart, absolutely. Otherwise, she'd be prey to anything that came along, wouldn't she?

"Would you like some toast with your scotch?" The voice came from behind him. She was leaning against the doorframe in her Springsteen nightshirt, a slightly rumpled, slightly gaunt middle-aged woman without make-up. This was how her intimates knew her. Give her a silk dress and ten minutes in any bathroom and you'd have yourself something altogether different.

"It was a rhetorical question," she said when he turned away without answering. And then the second beat sounded. "Nice morning."

"Yes," he answered.

The male was near the centre now, approaching steadily. He wondered what the signals were, what did he send to her through the strands? Are you okay love? Is the heat getting to you? Would it help if I rubbed your back for a while? Or was it just a dumb nothing, one creepy body moving toward another. When the eggs or the little live bodies came out, would either of them have any notion of context? Would they know what they'd done?

She disappeared from the doorway, he felt her go and after a time she returned with her toast, heaped high with strawberry conserve, and a strong black cup of last night's coffee. She could drink mud, this woman. She sat beside him on the tête-à-tête and put her plate on the wrought iron table between them, next to his glass. He wrapped his hand around his drink.

"God, I slept," she said.

"Good," he said. "I'm glad."

"So today the world is mine," she said.

"Good," he said. That was another thing this woman could do, sleep. It had scared the hell out of him the first time. They'd made love in a dingy hotel in some backwater town, the first time they'd been alone and free, and within seconds she was gone. He thought she'd lost consciousness, passed out, and he roused her and what? she asked, what's wrong? Nothing, he'd told her and she smiled and left him again, just as quickly. Now she could do it anytime; it no longer required his touch. An adaptation.

"Sally and I and the bridesmaids are going for a last fitting," she said. "At ten."

"What colour is your gown again?" he asked.

"It's ivory," she said. "They talked me into ivory. Mother of the bride elegance. But I'm holding out for a big peach hat."

"You should have a peach dress," he said, "if that's what you want. Peach would be nice on you."

"It's her day," she said. "And she's hot on ivory. She says there will be ten women my age in peach. Peach is too popular."

"I see," he said. He finished his drink.

"Are you ready for a coffee?" she asked.

"No," he said.

He didn't want to chance looking over at the spiders now. He went inside for another drink. Their daughter was at the sink, rinsing out a glass, pouring some orange juice into it.

"Good morning," she said.

"Hi pumpkin," he said. He walked up behind her and wrapped his arms around her waist, the glass still in his hand.

She didn't respond the way he hoped she would, hadn't for ten years. She looked down at his hands. "You and the scotch and the sun," she said. "Maybe we could get you an IV."

He dropped his arms and went to his bottle on the dining room buffet. He heard a muffled, "Sorry, Daddy," and returned to the kitchen as if nothing had happened.

"You're going for a fitting," he said.

"Want to come?" she asked. "You should come with us. I'm gorgeous in it."

He made a point of not taking a drink in front of her.

"I know it's all pretend," she said, "but I love this dress. I am a princess in this dress. It makes me want to twirl and stand up on my toes and curtsey low to someone." And she twirled and went up on her toes and curtsied low to him in her pyjamas.

"I can't imagine who you should curtsey to," he said. "Though you are a princess, you truly are." He thought he'd never seen her so beautiful as right then at the sink, not even when she emerged from her mother yawning and stretching and bawling in shock at the air on her brand-new skin. He wanted her to have her mother's old abandon, he wished it could be passed on to her like an heirloom, though he'd never tried to imagine her in anyone's arms. She did say she loved this boy she was about to marry. She said it a dozen times a day.

"Did your brother show any signs of consciousness?" he asked.

"None," she said. "Why?"

"I don't know," he said. "The grass needs cutting, I guess."

He didn't do any of the yard work himself anymore. He'd started a fire in the garage with the mower the previous spring and he'd been slow reacting to it, had got the shakes just watching the flames go up the wall. She'd smelled it and found him and they got it out and she threatened him for the first and only time. She was wearing her Springsteen nightshirt that morning too.

"Drink every minute of your life," she'd said. "Drink every God damned second. But don't kill us. I don't intend to die because you're drunk. That's not how I want to die. You don't touch anything flammable or sharp or electrical in this house again, you understand? You do and I'm gone. We're all gone."

So he didn't do anything dangerous. Their son did it all; he was old enough and he couldn't find any other work anyway that was worth his while, that was the line he used on his mother.

"He'll get up sometime," she said, holding the glass of orange juice against her temple. "He always does."

"Did he show up at that dance last night?" he asked.

"No, Dad, he didn't," she said.

"Just asking," he said.

She offered him the last of her orange juice, which he took, just the last inch, full of pith and a heavy sweetness. "He'll come out of it," she said.

"But when?" he asked. "This century?"

The boy drove an ancient Mercedes bike, which he had no idea how to fix, and his "lady" sported a tattoo of a fish on her taut left cheek, he had this by hearsay. There was a savings account, started when the boy was seven in Superman pyjamas, with thirteen thousand unused university dollars in it.

"Do you think little Pauline will be the next one to join our happy family circle?" he asked.

"Oh, Dad," she said.

"She could get knocked up like that," he said, snapping his fingers.

"Don't worry about what hasn't happened," she said. "Don't make stuff up." She emptied the coffee pot down the drain and refilled it with clear water. "Pauline's all right for now."

"For now?" he asked.

"You remember Grant?" she asked.

"I most certainly do," he said.

"Well he went away," she said. "I didn't get pregnant did I?"

He looked at his scotch, at the rich amber liquid, counting the things he'd never been told.

"How would I know?" he asked.

She dumped the old coffee grounds and poured new into the top of the machine. The smell nauseated him.

"Want some eggs?" she asked. "I'll make an omelette if you'll split it with me."

"No," he said. "Thanks. You make one though. Maybe your mother will have some. I'll ask her." He started down the few steps to the sunporch, stopping midway, turning back to her. "I have something to show you," he said quietly. "Maybe after your fitting, come sit with me."

She stood with the fridge door open, staring at the shelves, the light hitting her just under the chin. "Sure," she said. "Why not?"

His wife sat half turned in her chair, holding her empty coffee cup. She was watching the spiders. "Did you see them?" she asked. "What are they? What kind?"

He looked at them, as though for the first time. "Spiders," he said. "I don't know what kind." The sun was on the web now, fully. He sat down beside her. "Sally is willing to make an omelette if she can get a taker."

"Why would they be white?" she asked.

The girl appeared at the door. "You game for some omelette?" she asked.

"I've just had toast," her mother said, then, "Yes, all right, I'll have some. There's mushrooms. Whatever."

The girl turned away, juggling the two eggs she'd brought.

"So," he said. "A peach hat. A big peach hat."

"I think they're called wolf spiders," she said.

"How would you know that?" he asked.

"I'm going to kill them," she said.

"What?" he asked, knowing.

"I don't mind two," she said. "But there won't be two for long, will there?" She got up and walked past him into the house. He could hear cupboard doors banging and she came back around the corner holding the Black Flag, the heavy-duty green can, the one with the sketches of black heavy-duty insects, grasshoppers and slugs and roaches. Then she was out the screen door, closing it quietly behind her, her nightshirt transparent against the sun, aiming.

The male was with the female, his body partly covering hers, as if he could see the can and knew what was in it.

He closed his eyes and drained his scotch while she sprayed, he could hear nothing but the long, loud hiss.

"God but they're ugly," she said. Some of the spray was floating back into her face and she began to cough. She was losing patience. "They won't give up," she said, holding her finger firmly on the nozzle. Then, "Come on guys, off to spider heaven."

When it was done she came back into the sunporch and set the can beside his empty glass, still coughing, trying to get the last of the foul air out of her lungs.

Then, half-laughing, she offered, "I'm dying here." She looked toward the web to see if they'd dropped, not meaning to see his face at all.

And he held it back, just behind the wall his eyes made, for a steady two minutes. He knew without looking that the spiders hadn't moved. He knew the strands they'd made could hold dead weight, the centre strands particularly, for hours and hours.

"Please," she said. "Don't start."

Sister

"Would you stop the car?" she asked. The brother who sat at the wheel braked reluctantly.

"Don't do this," he said, waiting, adding, "you'll get drenched."

But he'd stopped the funeral procession, just yards short of the massive stone entrance to the cemetery. The mourners in the cars behind them might have thought there was a flat tire up ahead, or a stalled engine, though only the best cars were in the long slow line, Lincolns and Chryslers and Oldsmobiles; second cars, the ones more likely to have balding tires or engines past their prime had been left at home, in side yards. There were no limousines, this wasn't the city, but the funeral director, her long-ago chemistry partner, provided a late model, silver-grey hearse. Its smooth lines were not unlike the lines of the cars which had followed it through the town.

Her father, erect in the front seat, his head bowed in stiff continuous prayer, said nothing. At the service he'd stood on shaky legs responding in brave confusion to everyone who approached him offering sympathy, mistaking some of them, asking occasionally, "Do I know you?" He'd told all who would hear that he'd never dreamed he'd have to bury any of his children.

"Thank you," she said. And "I'm sorry."

She opened the door and climbed out. When the movement of cars began again, she stood on the side of the road at the edge of the ditch and waited for the procession to pass, her father's battered trenchcoat over her shoulders against the downpour. The orchard behind her was a vivid wet green, apples by the thousands glowed in the rain, pulling hard on the gnarled limbs of the trees. The ditch at her feet ran full downhill toward the cemetery; she watched the toads jump and skid on its slippery banks.

The cars rolled by, chock full of friends and relatives, front seats and back. She knew most of these people, or should have; some of them tried to catch her eye, their mouths ready with compassionate smiles, but none of them stopped. The car that did was from out of town. The window was rolled down by a woman who looked like Anne Bancroft.

"You're the sister," the woman said.

"Yes, I am," she answered.

"Would you like to ride with us?" she asked, the man beside her leaning forward in his seat, ready to reinforce the invitation.

"No," she said. "I'm walking. Thank you."

"We're all so sorry," the woman said, speaking with solid authority for everyone in the car.

"Yes," she answered. "It was good of you to come so far."

The woman nodded and rolled her window up and the car moved on through the entrance.

She remembered these people; they'd been at U of T with her brother, thirty years earlier. She remembered week-ends at the lake. They drove up from somewhere far away and she'd been only eight or nine. She remembered engagement rings on beautifully manicured hands, and halter tops, and fishing rods and boxes full of shiny blue spinners. And young men with short, cropped hair, one of whom cooked her marshmallows at the fire on the beach and kissed her good night. She remembered her brother bringing more wood for the fire, "borrowing" it from the neighbour's pile late at night. She could see him standing in the light thrown by his magnificent fire, his arms around a soft young blonde, grinning, saying, "Don't worry about the wood. There's lots of wood."

He hadn't been the first to die. He'd been a pallbearer in Ottawa the summer before, he'd told her this when she was sitting with him a month earlier. He said he'd been in the procession that time, not dead leading it.

The news of his cancer had moved from one person to another like a web connecting them. There were short, quiet discussions on the street and difficult phone calls made, one after the other, to those in other parts of the province, other parts of the country, like her. She'd asked, "Should I come now?" and they could only say it was up to her and she did come back to spend some time with him and then she'd had to go home and she'd phoned and phoned and they finally said, "You'd better come. You'd better come tomorrow."

And while they were all phoning and flying and driving and writing impossible notes, and sitting with him, quietly talking, and trying, without success, to console her father, who had never for a moment since he'd buried her mother believed he would not be the next to die, the cancer moved like a slimy bomb from her brother's bowel straight up his back to his brain, blowing up everything it passed.

She'd wanted cremation. She wanted each mad cell to go up in flames, but she didn't ask. Her family had never burned anyone. They were afraid of fire. It reminded them of Hell.

Standing on the edge of the ditch, he was alive beside her, wearing his yellow cardigan. His hair, grey and thick and curly, and his straight white teeth reassured her that what she'd done was perfectly reasonable. He laughed and threw his arm around her shoulders, pulling her off balance. "So you've bolted," he said, she heard it clearly and she relaxed against him. He turned her with his arm and they started off home. Then he disappeared, his reassurance gone.

She looked back toward the cemetery. She remembered sitting, swinging on the wrought iron gate; she could feel the top bar cutting into the back of her legs while she waited for her friends, never going in, never wanting any more fright than she'd been born knowing.

The cars moved through. The hearse had already reached the green awning at the grave site on the far side and people were beginning to climb out of cars and gather under and around it. Umbrellas, mostly black, one or two pastels, popped open. The aged were being helped across the uneven ground by the middle-aged and children were approaching on their own, joining the clusters that belonged to them, tucking into the arms of mothers and uncles. She saw her father go under the awning and the separation people made for his approach.

She heard her name and turned. A car she didn't recognize had stopped and a woman climbed out without looking at her, walked to the car behind and got in. There were only a few cars left, it was nearly over. She ducked her head to see the driver. "You're soaking wet," he said. "Get in."

When she didn't move he got out and ran around and put her in, wrapping the wet trenchcoat over her legs before he shut the door. He got in behind the wheel again, shaking the rain out of his hair, smoothing it. He turned the car around, forward and reverse, forward and reverse, stopping just short of the ditches, and then he touched her hand, lightly. Sitting in the car, she was surprised at the force of the rain.

"So you've bolted," he said.

— 83 —

She looked at him, at his thinning blond hair and his long full face. "I didn't see you at the service," she said.

"I was there," he said. "Everyone was there." He reached over and rubbed her cheek with the back of his hand. "I'm sorry," he said. "At least it was fast. He didn't have to go through years of it."

"Yes," she said. "At least it was fast." She unwrapped the trenchcoat. "I haven't seen you since my mother's funeral I guess. We should stop meeting this way."

He drove the car more slowly now that they were away from the cemetery. "Were you going to walk home? To your Dad's?"

"I don't know," she said.

"Is that where you want to go?" he asked.

"I don't want to go anyplace," she said.

He drove through the streets, past the churches and down the main drag and out to the highway and then back through the town to the other highway.

"We were always going someplace when we were kids," she said. "Where did we go? There's no place."

"There is for the kids," he said. "It's the same for them. The rink, the school, the creek, out into the country. They still go."

"How many did you end up with?" she asked.

"Four," he answered. "Three girls and a boy." He put his hand on the seat between them. "You look good," he said.

She turned her face to him, wanting him to see, clearly, how she really looked.

"I drive my kids everywhere," she said.

"How many?" he asked.

"Just the two," she said. "My two bouncing boys."

He was quiet as he drove past the gas stations again and turned around just beyond the tracks. "Someone said your husband left you," he said.

"Someone's right," she answered. "And that was your wife who got out of the car?"

"Yes," he said. "Judy."

"She was one of the Graham girls," she said. "She's her mother all over again, isn't she?"

He didn't answer.

"Does she do that often?" she asked.

"What?" he answered.

"There aren't many women who would give up their place in their husband's car."

"She's no dummy," he said.

She pulled the trenchcoat around her shoulders again. "That's something I'd never do."

He shrugged and adjusted the rearview mirror.

"Someone told me you own half the town," she said. "You've bought up everything your father lost and then some."

"Pretty much," he said.

"Are you rich then?" she asked. "Like he was when we were kids?"

"Your father co-signed my first three loans and I haven't had to look back," he said.

"I bet you're a Rotarian and all the rest of it," she said.

"No," he said. "You don't have to do that anymore."

"Too bad your Dad didn't live to see it," she said. "I liked him, you know. Except for the booze he was fine."

"We had to put him in the cheapest box we could get," he said. "You wouldn't remember. You were already gone to university. Not enough to learn here."

"I'm sorry," she said.

"When he had it he gave thousands to this town. Tens of thousands by today's dollar."

"I know," she said. "Everybody knows." They were passing a new subdivision on the outskirts of the town, houses where corn used to grow. "You own that?" she asked. "Those new split levels?"

"Yep," he answered. "You want one?"

She laughed for the first time in weeks. "No," she said. "Thanks anyway."

He drove silently again, wheeling around corners with one hand the way he used to when his other hand was on her. "What about the church?" he asked. "Do you want to show up?"

"It will be in the basement?" she asked.

"I imagine so," he said.

"There will be lots of tea," she said. "And good coffee. And salmon sandwiches and butter tarts. And all the old women who taught us what we'd need to know with their flannelgraphs, the parting of the Red Sea, and the coat of many colours, and the prodigal son, they'll be pushing lemon pie and angel food cake."

"Some of them are gone," he said.

"Yes," she said. "Of course they are. My father always tells me who is dead when he phones. But then I forget. Sometimes I ask about someone who's been gone for years. He tells me I should try to remember who is dead." She rolled her window down and stuck her hand out into the rain.

"Do you want to go?" he asked.

"Maybe for a while," she said. "I should."

He made a U-turn at the golf course and drove toward the red brick church. The streets were empty. Five o'clock and the streets were empty. Then she remembered where everyone was.

They came to the corner where the church stood and he drove around to the back and into the empty parking lot.

"We're the first," he said. He leaned across her lap and punched the button on the glove compartment. "Could you use a drink?"

She watched his hand, surprised. "You don't still drink in the car?" she asked.

He didn't answer.

"Good God," she said.

"I don't if I've got someone with me. The kids. And I never get drunk anymore." He took the bottle out and held it by the neck.

"You drink and you never get drunk," she said.

"That's right," he said. "Never the fool. Not anymore."

She turned away from him. "Cheaper than cocaine," she said.

"You don't use cocaine," he said. "Not a chance."

"No," she said. "No." She turned back to him and they checked each other for the old mockery. It wasn't there. Something without energy had replaced it, something in the no-man's-land between endurance and exhaustion.

"I could use a drink," she said.

He took two styrofoam cups from a clear plastic bag and handed them to her. She held them steadily while he poured.

"These are an improvement," she said. And then, in imitation of a forgotten teen-aged voice, "Just a little. If they smell it on me I'm dead."

He laughed. "Sorry, I don't carry mix anymore," he said.

"It makes me wince to think what they smelled on us," she said. "All the evils of the world on our breath and our clothes and our skin. And they had to wait up to smell it. Worried." She sipped at the warm rye, feeling it burn the back of her throat as it passed. "He taught me to drink scotch, you know. He caught me sick. I was maybe seventeen and he was home for a wedding and he found me outside after you'd dropped me off. He held me while I threw up into the peonies, he wasn't sober either, and he said, 'It's the mix. You've got to start drinking scotch.' He said, 'Tell that jerk to buy you scotch if he has to get you drunk.' " She rolled her window all the way down and put her face out into the rain. He watched her shoulders make the old moves. "He wasn't even fifty," she said.

"I'm sorry," he said and he reached over and pulled her away from the window toward him. But his hands were too heavy on her and she pulled away, back to the window.

He sat for a minute and finished his drink. "I went to see him half a dozen times over the last month," he said. "Lots of people did. He looked like hell but he was totally himself and he wanted company, lots of it. Everybody got to hear about you coming home to see him. He played it like a command performance."

He poured himself another drink and offered her the bottle, which she ignored. "That's not the first time the hearse has been to the cemetery since you left home," he said. "There've been many trips. It's a booming business for our friend Reg."

She remembered his nephew, a bantam hockey player in a car coming home from an away game. Her father had mentioned it in a letter.

"Yes," she said. "Of course it is."

She turned toward him and extended her cup, which he filled.

"They took him golfing last week," he said. "They put him in a cart and propped him up on the greens and he putted. Seven of them, fifty bucks a putt. They went all over the course, cut through the Americans like they owned the place." He threw back his rye and chuckled.

"I can imagine," she said and she did imagine it. She knew who his friends were: his lawyer, his accountant, the guys he used to curl with, the same guys who sat near the casket in the funeral parlour, one of them drunk, one in a MacKenzie kilt, their necks tense as they waited through the words to carry him out to the hearse on the street.

She tried to guess which of them would have held him while he putted and she decided each one would have taken a turn. There would have been at least one crude joke about them holding him up and he would have laughed with them and called them heartless bastards or something worse, something really low down and vile and hilarious. She wondered if he carried his silver flask, they all had them, and if there was Cutty Sark in his, or morphine.

She sat up straight and sipped at her drink.

The lot was beginning to fill with cars, in no particular order. Through the rain streaming down the windshield she could see cousins and second cousins and old neighbours and cronies of her father's, one with a walker. Most of her mother's friends would be inside, standing over pots of tea.

"How do you feel?" he asked.

"Not quite ready," she said. She saw all the women at her mother's funeral, gathering around her and hugging her one after the other and patting her back and then asking about her children. "The women," she said. "I don't think I'm up to it."

"You're still too hard," he said. "They can't help it. They look at you they see a ten-year-old."

"I know," she said. "I'm just not very grateful."

"No," he said. "You're not." He turned the ignition. "There's your Dad," he said. "God, he looks old."

"I never, ever imagined him," she said, "as old as he is today."

"Mine didn't live long enough," he said. "And yours is living longer than he wants to. Jesus."

"He wants me to come home," she said. "When he bought the plot for today he bought three more, for the rest of us. Right behind Mom. He doesn't see why that won't work. So we had to say, yes, thanks Dad."

"You won't come home?" he asked.

"How could I come home?" she asked. "Most of my life has been somewhere else."

He screwed the lid back on the bottle and laid it carefully in the glove compartment, put the car into reverse and backed out of the lot. He drove down the front street again and at the end of it he cut back into the junk-filled alley behind the stores. He parked on a gravel flat behind the hardware store, overlooking the tracks.

"I'm going to show you something," he said.

They got out of the car and ran through the rain to an old wooden door, the key for which he had on a large ring in his suit pants pocket. The first key he tried didn't work so he tried another and she pulled the trenchcoat up over her head and then they were inside, in a dark back room. There were cases of chisels and paint brushes and screws piled around them, some half empty, some still taped shut. He opened an inside door and they walked up a flight of stairs. On the landing at the top of the stairs he found another key and opened the last door and then he stepped back and she went in ahead of him.

"You've made it into an apartment," she said.

"Just finished," he said. "One of the school teachers wants it."

She walked through the rooms. There was a modern kitchen, it even had a microwave, and two bedrooms, one furnished, one empty. In the living room a tan sofa and chair sat on a Flokati rug. The picture window overlooking the street had no drapes, only a scalloped blind, half pulled. She remembered being sent up here for boxes of nails and pliers when she worked for Mr. Rawlings after school and on Saturdays. She remembered the hazy light coming in through the filthy window summer and winter and the boxes stacked all over the floor and the mouse dirt everywhere she looked.

"This is where we used to grope," he said.

"Doesn't Mr. Rawlings need it for storage anymore?" she asked.

"Mr. Rawlings hasn't had the hardware store for ten years," he told her. "I built a shed across the alley for the new guy. It's cleaner and handier."

"Did Mr. Rawlings die?" she asked.

"Mr. Rawlings lives in Florida with his second wife," he said. "He's like you. He never comes back."

"I come back," she said.

"No you don't," he said.

She walked over to the window. She could see the church, its grey roof and the steeple with the bell. The whole town looked clean, she thought, and properly laid out, if you looked at it from a good angle. It looked like a TV shot of a New England town, without the flag. She felt his hand on her shoulder, resting there, not seductive at all.

"Did you love him?" she asked.

"Love him?" he said.

"Did he make a difference to you? Were you glad he was alive?"

He walked to the couch and stretched out on it, throwing his feet up over the end, exposing the barely worn soles of his brogues. "You don't know anything about what went on here in the last few years," he said. "You don't even ask the right questions. People have been dying, kids have been born. You wouldn't know my kids if you saw them on the street, you've never even seen them. Things change. Your brother changed."

She kept her back to him. "In what way did he change?"

"Well," he said. "Nobody was very impressed when he walked out on his wife and kids."

"His kids were nearly grown," she said. "There were problems. He had to leave."

"Nobody has to leave," he said.

"I don't see that it's anyone's business what he did," she said.

"But it is," he said. "Maybe not where you come from, but it is here. Things overlap here."

"Were there teams?" she asked. "Her team and his?"

"Yeah," he said. "There were teams."

"And whose were you on?" she asked.

"She had no money," he said. "She was forty-three years old and she had to go hunting for a job."

"Which she was fully capable of doing," she said. "She got the house. She's survived. She was at the service."

"Yeah," he said. "She was at the service."

"You don't have to worry about her any more," she said. "I'm one of his executors. She's going to get what she's entitled to."

"That's not my point," he said.

"Men shouldn't leave?" she asked. "Is that your point? Is that your mean little standard? Your wife climbs out of the car so another woman can climb in but she can count on you, is that it?"

"Yeah," he said. "That's it."

"Bully," she said.

"Bully to you," he said. He got up and went into the kitchen, returning with an unopened bottle of rye and two wine glasses.

"I bet the school teacher is a woman and I bet you were saving that for her," she said, watching him pour. He didn't answer. "I'm right," she said.

"You can't ever let up," he said. "The school teacher is just a kid."

"I'll bet she is," she said. "A real sweet kid." She took the glass he offered. "He owed you money, didn't he? You're the big shit now and he owed you. He owed a lot of people from what I hear."

"That doesn't matter to anyone now," he said. "Let's just let him rest."

"Well you'll all get your money," she said. "He carried more than enough insurance."

"That was his problem," he said. "Always more than enough. That's what he turned into. Cadillacs, ladies, real estate. He had it all. More than enough but not all paid for."

"Shut up," she said.

"Things go wrong," he said.

"Oh do they?" she asked. "How bloody surprising."

She stood looking out, banging her glass on the window, staring at the church.

"Last month when I was home," she said, "I went to church. Dad asked me to go with him and I went. My first Communion Sunday in twenty years." She took a drink, held the rye in her mouth and eased it down, bit by bit. "He sat there holding the cup in his spotted old hand and then he lifted it to his mouth, fast, the way he always has, and he choked. On grape juice."

He was on the sofa again, but sitting up this time, leaning forward over his wine glass.

"Some woman in the pew ahead of us turned around and told him to put his arms up over his head so he sat there with his arms like this," and she showed him the position of surrender, "choking. And what I wanted to do was put my arms up with him so he wouldn't look so foolish but I couldn't. All I could do was stare at the empty cross up over the minister's head and wish he could stop, wish it was over." She emptied her glass. "Fifty years in that church believing and it always got him what he wanted. But not that day." She set her glass on the window sill. "Do you think maybe he should have gone to his knees? Or flat out, what's the word, prostrate?"

He didn't answer.

"Blood of Christ," she said.

"Easy," he said, getting up, approaching the window.

"I'm not done," she said. "That afternoon, after I fried Dad his eggs and he went for his nap, I drove over to sit with Rob. He wasn't having a very good time. People were coming and going and he was trying hard but he was hurting, he was into the morphine. It was liquid, the doctor gave it to him in liquid, to take home."

"I know," he said.

"He told me to get the Welch's from the fridge and I did, I handed him the whole bottle. He said it was the only thing that would kill the taste of the morphine. He said morphine tasted God awful and he said he hoped I'd never have to know how bad it tasted. He had a little plastic cup —"

"I know," he said.

"— marked off in centimetres and he poured the morphine to the half-way mark and he topped it up with Welch's and he threw it back."

She was suddenly cold and she shrugged the damp trenchcoat off her shoulders and rubbed her fleshy upper arms with her open hands.

"Can you believe that?" she asked. "I'm almost tempted to believe. A punch drunk old God watching every move we make."

She said this last against his chest, leaning into him. He stood rocking her for a long time.

When she was over it she said, "You loved me a whole hell of a lot, didn't you?"

"It doesn't stop," he said, ready to pull away.

She brought her hand to her blouse and unbuttoned it and when she was finished she put both hands on his buttocks, which, she was surprised to discover, she remembered, exactly. They began the way they did when they were young, and she waited until he had passed the point of no return, until she was sure, and then she asked again, "Did you love him?"

Landscape

Edgar and I signed the papers on this property forty years ago, when the boys were tots. We agreed on a ten-year plan for the house and we carried it out to a large extent, fixing things as we had the money. But we landscaped immediately. Before we married we'd bought a gardening book full of botanical names and wonderful pictures in readiness for the time when we would have our own place. We worked together. We built the arbours and the fence and the garden shed, for the tools. We pruned correctly and trained the growth and we were rewarded. Everything we planted grew strong and lush and thrived almost without us.

In the very beginning, the yard held just the two magnificent red maples. The tree house, built with odd planks criss-crossed according to the boys' shared vision of what a tree house should be, is still there, up in the far one. I can't see it for the leaves but I suspect it is rotten by now. Here beside me, the horse chestnut dominates the yard, brazenly unaware of its own ugliness, outshowing even the maples. I can't look at it without hearing the English boys. They lived down the street for a couple of years and they came to me their first summer, carrying rakes and full grins, asking if they could knock the conkers out of my tree. They giggled together at my lack of comprehension and pointed to the chestnut. I let them do it and I paid them two quarters each to rake up the leaves they'd brought down. Edgar laughed and said it was perverse but I loved their clear voices in the yard. It was worth a bit of silver.

I could pull a kind laugh from him so easily when I was young and strong. All I had to do was wake up in the morning.

As well as the chestnut, we planted a hickory nut, near the back fence; we have gathered its harvest every year for my Christmas baking. At the arbour, behind the garage, we put a dozen lilacs, the kind that sucker and spread, and near them, the pussy willow. Edgar threatened to cut it down when the boys were small and wouldn't stop shoving the buds up their nostrils but they knew he meant business and they stopped pretty smartly. He was good with them when they were little. There was just the one bed, for the roses, the proper roses. The tea roses, we trained along the fence where it meets the side of the house, trained them up over the trellis above the gate. Our gesture of welcome. My children brought me roses, all of them, as soon as they were old enough to avoid the thorns. John especially. And he often brought me the porcelain rose bowl from the buffet. He liked to watch as each arrangement took its shape.

We had high hopes for the fish pond but there were too many boys, too many footballs and fly balls splashing in. Edgar said the fish were nervous wrecks so we stopped stocking it. Eventually we filled it just for the pleasure of the sky's reflection.

Today it looks like a curving grave.

It's not pleasant sitting here in the ruin, waiting for him to show up.

Two of our sons are gone. They live in other provinces. We do see them when they come for their visits but it's not the same as having them come slamming in the back door, wanting something. But they have families and careers and we are proud of them.

John is closer. Every month or so I take the bus into the city where he works and after I've spent my pension on the distant grandchildren I meet John for dinner. He always chooses some elegant place and he orders me things I've never heard of and he always pays the bill. He tells me outrageous tales about modern day life and I make sure I am never shocked. I appreciate the effort he makes to help me adjust to the world as it is now. I could never manage it on my own. What I like best is watching his perfect white teeth, which he got, if I may say so, from me.

It hurt me more than a little that I was never invited to his home but now I know why and there's no reason to feel that way. He came last Sunday and we sat here at this picnic table, Edgar and John and I, and he spilled it. John has a lover and his lover does not feel comfortable with straight people.

My lover; that's what he said. I was holding my coffee in mid-air when he said it and I did take my love away from him, I'll admit that, but I swallowed the word with my coffee and I gave the love back. His friend is older, an accountant I think, his lover. John was leaning into my shoulder when he said the proper word for it, to help us I suppose, and I was reminded, just for a half-second, of the botanical words Edgar and I used to study when we were planting. Edgar didn't like the word. He got up from the table and moved away, leaving only his pronouncement: "Your mother and I are heart-broken." So dead sure. We watched him go around the corner of the house to the garden shed.

A long time ago we used to have what Edgar called fun in that shed. We did the potting and the sharpening and I brought trays of coffee and cookies which we ate in the quiet dark evenings after the boys were asleep in their beds. We talked and touched and laughed and shushed each other. I assumed when he put the heater in and started to go out to it alone that he needed some privacy away from the chaos of raising three boys. I know now that that was the time when I should have done something, though I can't imagine what I could have done.

I did go to the shed last Sunday, after John left. I was ready with the speech of my life but when I opened the door and saw him sitting there, leaning back against the raw wood wall with his arms crossed, ready to counter whatever I could think of to say, I was stopped by a picture of him dead. He was so rigid. I didn't know where to touch him.

I feel responsible. When we were young together, Edgar's firm opinions calmed me. Though he took a long time about it, he could separate things and weigh them and come down firmly on one side or the other. It was something I had trouble doing and with Edgar, I felt secure. I believed he had a kind of strength.

The hardening has crept up on us and I have tried to deny it. I know that happens. And my efforts to stop it weren't nearly good enough. I could have done more the first time, with Becky's baby. His own niece, caught young, with a baby on her hands. She came to us in trust, sharing her waiting time and she brought the infant to us right from the hospital, giddy with the bundle in her arms.

"Where is the father?" Edgar asked. Just like that. Becky left immediately, of course, holding the child tight against her old duffle coat. Edgar slammed out the back door, and later, when he came in from the shed I asked him what he thought he was pulling. "Sit down, woman," he said. "Sit down and listen to me." He said he cared a great deal for Becky and I said that's news and he said hush and he told me that society was falling down all around us and it was because no-one insisted on anything anymore. He said bastard children didn't have a chance. I should have made him hold it. I should have said it was my house too and if I wanted to have bastard children in it, I would, he could watch.

Becky never came back and that was eighteen years ago. I know because I send a fancy dress each birthday. I remember her nursing that child, so confidently and well. I remember how the feeling came back to my own breasts as I sat on the bed watching.

There is no pattern to the occurrences. They happen once a year, twice a year, with no nasty mood to hint that something's going to happen, to give a person time to prevent. Often it's sheer silliness. This past winter, the hockey team he supports forgot to invite him to their wind-up banquet. Only a mother with tired eyes, I told him, jotting out invitations, forgetting your name for no reason but carelessness. They phoned him during dessert to ask where he was but he said he couldn't come. He threw on his parka and he went to the shed. Last Sunday, it would have been better for all of us if I'd found him sobbing there.

I can hear Agnes on the chimes at the Presbyterian church. She lost her husband last October but she keeps on.

Edgar's been to the lawyer. John is out of the will. Not a nickel, not a dime is going to get into the hands of some strutting, simpering idiot who doesn't have the strength to fight his own weakness. That's what he said. John does not strut or simper. He is strong and graceful. Not, I swear, unlike his father.

On Tuesday, Edgar fertilized the roses and I helped him. Then he organized the shed and I helped him do that. We emptied it and took inventory. I watched while he hosed it down and we had tea and cookies while he aired it. I brought him his tools to sharpen.

That evening he left to go to the city. I knew there was a conference on and I knew he'd been invited, as he has been since his retirement, I just didn't think he'd go. I don't know how he could. But I did up his shirts and waved him off. He promised me he'd come home yesterday.

I knew in the back of my mind that he'd see John and I knew I couldn't give any warning. So many things an old woman can't do. When John made his Sunday call this morning, I wasn't going to interfere at all and then I couldn't stop myself. I asked.

Edgar told him he'd broken the bond. He said it was irrevocable.

I told John I'm coming for supper next Friday night. I told him to tell his friend that I'm coming for supper. I've got the address, I'll get a cab. He asked if he could phone me back but I said no. His friend can avoid me for a while if he must but I'm not going to avoid him. Not if he loves John. And it's my job to believe he does.

I'm not listening to the radio this morning. I couldn't possibly concentrate. I usually like to listen to "Sunday Morning" with the atlas John bought me so I can know which countries are where now. I told him I sometimes think a person can know too much about what's going on in the world and he said not you Mom. That's how much he loves me.

But Edgar loves me more. However much he's hardened, he still loves. I believe he does.

When I was in the shed getting the axe, Edgar's old plaid jacket hanging on the wall nearly stopped me. Guilt, I suppose.

I had a time getting started. I don't kid myself that things are easy anymore. I took the hickory nut first because it had the thinnest trunk. I didn't want to get myself worn out and have to stop half-way. It came down easily enough, as did the pussy willow. The lilac trunks resisted all the way through. That's where I got most of these scrapes. I couldn't get the chestnut down, I'm not surprised, but I've done enough damage that we'll have to get someone who does that sort of thing in to finish it off. The roses I simply smacked through at the base, all of them. The fish pond is overflowing with what I could manage to haul. Only the maples stand undamaged.

The signs of death are slow to work their way through a plant. Every rose I see and the leaves, thousands of them, are still strong and lush. It would be nice if there was someone to bring me a glass of iced tea. I'm all sweaty and I can feel the scrapes stinging now that I'm finished. I see a few of them are still bleeding. I should change my stockings.

I've had time to imagine what Edgar will say.

He's never called me anything but "woman" in anger but he'll call me something new this time. He'll call me something almost unbearable and then he'll say, "What you've done is irrevocable." He'll say, "We won't live long enough to do it all again."

"No," I'll tell him. "We won't."

Reflections

He calls her Mother and she calls him Dad. They have separate bedrooms. They begin each day by saying good morning when they meet in the kitchen for breakfast, fully dressed. In their nightclothes, they are an embarrassment to each other. If they happen to meet on the way to the bathroom before breakfast, there is no acknowledgement. For forty-seven years they have lived together. He sometimes tries to remember a time when it was not like this, but that time is gone.

They have come here to the cemetery at her insistence, to locate their plots. There's not much to face together any more, but there is this one thing. Or two things if you count each death separately. One of them, he knows, will go first, will have just the one death. But the other will have to go through two. The only thing worse would be a son or daughter going, dying, before them. He winces at the thought. He knows he doesn't have the strength, could never find the strength, to bury any of the children. He's seen a couple of friends do it, right here in this cemetery and it was worse than torture to watch. He and Mother buried one, a long time ago, but it was just an infant and they were young and had the other kids and the promise of more. No. One death, possibly two, that's all he could manage now.

He parks the Olds on the overgrown edge of the grass by the barbed wire fence. She gets out as if she's anxious to see what's ahead, checking her small flowered notebook for the instructions she got from the town clerk this morning. He sits in the car a minute, his big brown arm hanging out the window. He surveys the rows of massive old maples surrounding the place. There is room for shafts of sunlight to move through the maples, and his eyes follow them to the faces of the tombstones, where they explode. "What a bloody waste of sunlight," he mutters.

She's already thirty yards away. She motions with her arm for him to follow, doesn't turn, just keeps walking, one hand holding the notebook, the other waving him on. He watches the cardigan sweater responding to the swinging of her hips. He's never told her about the swinging of her hips.

He dreams her young with a waist so small he can wrap his hands around it. She is quiet and astoundingly elegant in a cloche hat and a mauve dress that reminds him of a meadow. Only her shoes are practical, sensible. She is a quiet mauve cloud, and he has to assume when she doesn't say no that she means yes.

He opens the heavy car door, thinks about a heart attack. That's what's most likely for him now. Two out of four brothers have gone that route already. A stroke would be all right as long as he doesn't live through it, doesn't find himself alive without a mind, or movement or speech. He shuns all other possibilities. He thinks of young people when he thinks of cancer. Leukemia, lung cancer, those are for the young.

By the time he catches up to her, she has stopped in front of a red stone. Before she can speak, he reads it, sees that it's Geordie Arnott for God's sake, Geordie Arnott who damned near got to her before he did, when they were young. Him with his manners and his soft womany voice. He charges on past her toward the area of the cemetery where their plots are supposed to be, where the leaves blow freely across the open expanse of grass.

He can't imagine what will take her. She's always been so small, so vulnerable, like a young calf. But nothing ever hurt her much. She had four of the kids right on the kitchen table, so many years ago now that it seems to him she just stopped ironing or scrubbing, jumped up on the table when the doctor came, went to bed for a day or two, then carried right on ironing or scrubbing. He has to admit he's no authority on those times. She would go into herself, and then the baby would take her until it could toddle around alone, sit at the table with them. And by then there would be another.

He dreams a child in woollen soakers with lovely fat thighs. He calls the child Pudge, and his eyes water as he heaves him high in the air over his head, thinking how solid, how strong, how God damned miraculous this thing is.

He continues to walk, turns and walks backward toward their plots. She is pausing here and there, reading inscriptions, pulling her cardigan tight around her small frame. She is pulling weeds away from the base of a stone he should recognize, but doesn't. It's a friend, he just can't remember which one.

Five years. If he was a betting man, he would put money on them both being dead within five years. The same span of time their sons are counting on to get their houses paid off, their pensions fattened up. No ignoring it. All you have to do is look around downtown, count the faces that were there last year and aren't there now. Lord knows he's had his suit out often enough in the last few years, and it hasn't been for christenings. The doctor says he has to stop thinking this way, has to stop dwelling on it. Says he should eat a little less too, and give up hauling the firewood in from the bush, as if it's all the same kind of thing.

Stop dwelling on it. Sure thing. He wishes he could take the doctor to that picture they saw last month when their daughter took them to the gallery in the city. It was a horse on some railroad tracks, and behind him, coming at him, was a train, a dark ugly iron-horse. The neck muscles were the biggest he'd ever seen on a horse, strained one against the other, not knowing whether to put their force into moving forward or looking back. And the hooves of that animal were suspended in the air, all four of them, and you just knew he'd never get his footing, never be able to dig in and get the hell out of the way of that thing bearing down on him. And he felt for that horse, knew how it was for that horse, could barely make himself look at the eyes painted on the face of the beast. He knew how wild they'd be. If he could get the doctor there, in front of that painting, he'd tell him to tell the horse to stop dwelling on that train, the noise of it, the force of it, coming down on him from behind. He'd tell the doctor if the horse agreed, he'd agree.

He is in the new area now, leaning against one of the maples that shades it. He looks back to the rows and rows of tombstones, and if she were not among them, wandering around, he would easily see the cemetery grow out in all directions, reproduce itself a hundred times and become a memory of those other cemeteries.

He dreams a war and a young man. The young man rides in the back of a truck. Bumping around beside him are guns and two dead friends. He is screaming with pain, but the bombs continue anyway and the shrapnel rains around him. The truck stops, and someone comes to him and rams a needle in his ass and ahh . . . this is morphine and it feels so good, feels so much better than the slow leaking away of his blood. Because he doesn't want it to leave, not all of it.

She's a lot more practical about death. She went over to the town clerk this morning, bought these plots for them, like twin beds. And last week she went to the tombstone dealer and chose their stone, had it engraved with their names and the dates of their births. She took him over when it was finished, made him look at it, but all he could see was the spaces for the dates still to be chiseled into the granite. She wanted him to pay for it then and there, but he told them to bill him. He'd be damned if he'd stand over his own tombstone and write out a cheque for it. It took him a long time to forgive her that little practicality, and now here they are, pretending that choosing the plot of land that will be dug up for them and thrown back over them is like choosing the damned house when they moved into town from the farm. Sometimes he suspects the blood runs cold through her small body, cold and thin, never slowing, never thickening with warmth for a minute. He knows this isn't fair, caught on a long time ago that it's no use hating her for what she seems to be doing or saying, no use judging her in any ordinary way. You just have to trust her, take the air she gives you and warm it yourself before you breathe it in.

Two of the kids have her way about them: the daughter who will never look at you or touch you, the son who turns everything to ice with his analyses. It broke his heart when he first saw it. But he loves them none the less, treats them equally with the others. And he's locked away on velvet cushions in his mind all the happy times with them, because they were so few.

She's coming over to him now, her head down, her steps on the path determined. He dreams a bride on his arm with the face of his wife, but her waist is thick with a grandchild for him. "The Wedding March" booms around them and he can feel her arm shaking in his as they start down the aisle, but she will not look at him, will not acknowledge that they are together in any way.

He moves away from the maple and stands behind her, reading the notebook over her shoulder, and he feels the blood leave his head. 1038 and 1093, what the hell kind of joke is this? But she is laughing, saying she just copied it down wrong, telling him to watch for the numbers on the stakes that are pounded into the ground at regular intervals. "Shit!" he shouts, taking an awkward old man's run at the line of stakes, kicking at them as he goes; shit, snap, shit, snap, until only one or two are left whole. The jagged splints expose fresh light-coloured wood. He feels winded and content. She ignores him. She bends over one of the stakes, pieces it back together so she can read the number on it. "Just settle yourself," she says.

Three of the kids have his way about them. They've always brought a madness, a spur of the moment kind of nonsense to everything that goes on, and he grins at the thought of them. They live full throttle. They have ups and downs more interesting than the ones he watches on the soaps every day. But the other two, she and the other two, live in some place that never changes, some place you couldn't find if you spent your whole life looking.

He dreams a search through cobwebs, through dust and dry stale air. He doesn't know what he's looking for and he wishes he had some help.

He tried to tell her about this one night when they were in the same warm bed together, but she cried, said he frightened her with his demands. Said she didn't live any place that ordinary people didn't live, and couldn't he just see it as her way of getting through things. She said you could roar and jump around and laugh out loud or you could do it all privately, to yourself. He understood then for a little while, was willing to call what he felt "understanding". And he tried to pull her to him, but she pulled away and cried more, had to leave the bed to get herself settled down.

"Here we are," she says, and he storms back across the cemetery, careless of his path, walking obstinately over graves, cheerfully patting tombstones as he swings himself around them, thinking not yet we aren't, not yet.

He slams the car door shut behind him and watches her approach. She is calm, her feet plant themselves in the exact centre of the dirt path. She is looking in his direction but the sunlight is coming right at the windshield and he can't tell if she sees him. Maybe she's looking at the reflection of the light; she would notice that, and like it. He holds his hand up to his brow to shade his eyes but it's no good.

In a few minutes she is beside him in the car, doing up her seat belt, tucking her notebook into her purse. He does not say he is sorry, he stopped saying he was sorry years ago. She would only respond, you should be, the anger in the words, never in the soft perfect face.

He dreams her at the bedroom mirror, an old woman in her nightgown, with her back to him. His eye catches the still small outline of her waist, and he can see the freckled shoulders clearly, but her face will not form itself. He sees the children's faces fading in and out of focus where hers should be, and once he sees his own face there, but never hers. He longs to gently mould the features, make her come alive for him, but he can't approach her. He is tangled in the messy, rumpled bed.

And they will die soon, he knows, and he can see three of the kids standing over the grave, hating it, as they should, raging. The other two will be dull-faced, doing whatever they are doing privately, to themselves.

If it is to be her standing with the children over his grave, she will be quiet and controlled, maybe admiring the damned tombstone. And he will be floating somewhere above them, somehow absolved by the grief of the grieving, somehow abandoned by the silence of the others.

But if it is to be him standing with them over her grave, he will sense her in the air around him, holding him, he will feel her final silence and he will go mad with missing her, mad with it.

He calls her Mother and she calls him Dad. They have separate bedrooms. They begin each day by saying good morning when they meet in the kitchen for breakfast, fully dressed. In their nightclothes they are an embarrassment to each other. If they happen to pass on the way to the bathroom before breakfast, there is no acknowledgement. For forty-seven years they have lived together. She sometimes tries to remember a time when it was not like this, but that time is gone.

She has finally got him down to the cemetery to locate their plots. It wasn't something she particularly wanted to do alone. But truth be told they will both die soon. First one, then the other. It can't be avoided. She supposes, has always supposed, that there is something after death, something for the energy, the spirit, to become. She has always supposed too that the child they buried long ago exists still somehow. It makes no difference that she can't imagine how or where. It is nice to dream that he has been all this time in someone's arms, that he will be shown to her, returned to her, but she knows that to be a foolish dream. A perfect leaf drifts down from one of the maples edging the cemetery, lands on her shoulder, sticks to the wool of her cardigan. She picks it off, takes the hard stem in her fingers and twists it, watching the colour spin. He's still in the car. She wishes he wouldn't brood so. She's so tired of all the dramatic phrases: six feet under, three score and ten, final resting place, and on and on. That's the talk at home, and now they're here, right in the middle of everything, he's got nothing to say.

She doesn't look back, just waves him on, knowing he'll be watching her to see if she'll do it. Then she hears the car door open, pictures his big frame emerging from the car. It's always reminded her of one of those clowns getting out of a little red circus car. He doesn't shut the door.

She dreams him young again with shoulders so wide they make her believe in him. He is all movement and strength, all power and lust and confidence. He makes her feel like a ripe garden peach pulling a branch to earth with the weight of its juice. And she is not afraid of his teeth, not yet.

She feels the pull in her groin as she walks, slips her hand under her cardigan to rub it. She's got to see about it. It's been going on too long. She blocks from her mind the picture of the organs she knows to be inside her there, doesn't want to know the particulars. If this small constant pain is to be the beginning of her dying, that's fine, she'll handle it the best she can. She'll see about it.

To her left, in the old part of the cemetery, half-way down the slope to the corn field beyond, rest her parents and her son. She won't go down today. One thing at a time. They're here on business. She does notice a beautiful marble stone three or four in from the path, and she goes over to it. It's pinkish in the sunlight, and she can see her image reflected in it, clear as day. He's almost beside her, and she thinks it would be nice to be reflected together on a warm autumn day like this, but he's gone, charging off like some mad old bull. Then she reads the inscription and sees it's Geordie Arnott. Surely he wouldn't think she was standing here mooning over Geordie Arnott. He had been a lovely suitor, but he didn't turn out all that well and Dad couldn't think she would trade her life for life with Geordie, not hardly. But he's off, mad about something that's nothing more than nonsense.

He will have a heart attack, she is sure. He's got too heavy since he gave up the farm, won't quit eating like an adolescent. She could spank him. If she doesn't cook potatoes, he invites her for a walk after supper, steers them directly to the new drive-in restaurant and wolfs down a double order of those greasy french fries. And since she's stopped baking pies and cakes, he's fallen head over heels in love with Sara Lee. Her eyes clamp shut at the image of him clutching his chest, bellowing in pain. She will call the ambulance and hold his hand as tight as she can, but it won't be enough, it won't stop anything.

She notices another stone, Laura Blain's. Born 1908. Died 1943. Half a life. They went through the baby years together. She shakes her head to get the thoughts out of it. There are weeds around the base of the stone, and she pulls them up, every one of them, by the roots.

She remembers the pain of having the children. Knows it was nothing, nothing like what the pain of death might be. But it hurt, just the same. And she remembers the doctor's eyes, challenging her to bear the pain, and she did bear it, would not have screamed out if it had killed her, partly to show what she was made of, but more because she was worried about the child being rammed through her pelvis. She could see the unborn baby, small and quivering, terrified at the force being used against it, unaware of the light ahead.

She dreams a child in woollen soakers with skin that seems to melt under her touch, it's that soft. She laughs at her own pleasure in handling him. And he is brave like his father, not afraid of stairs or cars or dogs or fire. She feels a tug of pride in his confidence, but still she has to teach him that he is not invincible, share some of her own fear with him so he will know when to back away from things.

Straightening up now, she sees him over by the fence, leaning against the trunk of a maple tree. His arms are folded across his chest, and he's kicking at the leaves absently. She wonders how many more autumns will come for them, how many more seasons. Four times five, four times four, four times three? She knows she must never count them out for him. He's reacting so badly to things, made a terrible scene at the gallery last month, in front of that painting. She was mortified. He says he's going to tell the doctor about that horse, to help him understand how a man feels. He'll be lucky if he doesn't get himself a prescription for Valium. She knew immediately what the painting might mean for him, but it was too late. She had to stop herself from exploring the horrors of the thing. Instead she looked at the frame, thought it would be better a little wider, mentioned this to their daughter. The girl threw her head back in exasperation, huffed away in a display almost equal in intensity to her father's.

She starts walking through the rows of stones toward him. She dreams him gone to war. There are two children at her feet and she is knitting socks. The children ask if the socks are for daddy, and she says yes they are, knowing full well that thousands of socks are being knitted at this moment, and that thousands of feet are cold and bleeding somewhere, and that it doesn't much matter which socks go on which feet. The faster she knits, the better the chance his feet will be warmed. She thinks only of his feet.

She notices a stone much like the one she chose last week for them. The bill for it came this morning. He tossed it across the table at her, said it gave him the chills. She isn't sorry, though, isn't sorry they are here today finding their plots. It wouldn't be right to leave it for the children to do. She's seen the children of friends over their parents' graves, and she marvelled at the quiet bond between them. A bond made of ordinary things like memories and shared houses and just the same last name. She doesn't want practicalities to spoil that bond for their own children.

They find themselves at funerals on a regular basis now. She has to keep a small supply of tarts and loaves in the freezer. At the funeral parlours he hugs whoever comes to him for hugging, mostly kids he's watched grow from infancy to middle age. And he watches the ones who don't come to him, watches them for signs, reflections of his own feelings.

Three of their own kids are great huggers, and they have his other ways about them too. They rage and roar around, have done so from the time they could first hold their balance as toddlers. It's never solved anything, but you couldn't tell them that. They court chaos. Still, they're good to have around, in moderate doses. When they're happy they bring everyone into it, like dancers pulling more partners to the floor.

She dreams a child who has failed a year at some far-off university. He is incensed at the injustice he has been served. She suspects he has been lazy and that he will be able to admit this to himself eventually, but first there must be a three-act play exploring his feelings about the failure. He charges from one side of the stage to the other, playing to her, watching for her reaction. But she gives none. She can neither laugh nor cry and she will not applaud. It's his play and his alone. She knows nothing about the theatre.

Where's the page now, where's the page with their plot numbers? She leafs through the notebook, turns past the birthday section and the anniversary section. The notes she took this morning are at the back, under P, for plot.

The other two kids are more like her. She is comfortable with them. They seem content with their lot and have been a help to the others in an ordinary, stable way. She does regret there is so little between them and their father, wishes they could meet his warmth with something of their own.

She dreams a party. Everyone but her and two of the children seem to be drunk with something, and they are dancing around, clapping their hands high above their heads and stomping, circling the three of them tighter and tighter. She senses there is some special thing they could do to escape, and she asks the others if they know what it is, but they don't. She thinks maybe they are expected to join the dancing and she tries, but her rhythm is off. She feels frightened and very foolish.

She is with him now, near the plots. He stands behind her, reading the notebook over her shoulder. She points to the numbers, 1038 and 1093 and she feels his terror on her neck. She laughs and says she copied it down wrong, of course it's 1039, 1038 and 1039. She asks him to watch for the numbers marked on the stakes pounded into the ground at regular intervals. And he's off, like an old maniac, he's swearing, running down the row of stakes, kicking at them, cursing, breaking them off, crack, crack, crack, huffing and puffing and half-tripping. Sometimes she suspects he doesn't have blood running through his veins at all, but lava, lava spilling out from some exploding core. Maybe that's where the heat comes from. He gives off a heat that exhausts, exhausts and frightens, because it can damage more than stakes. "Just settle yourself," she says.

She knows she should move back into their bedroom, even if he hasn't asked her to. The day she moved her clothes over to the other bedroom, he asked what the hell was going on, but when she tried to explain he got her sewing shears and cut one of her good Christmas nighties to pieces. Then he left, left the back door banging in the wind against the wall of the house. She was firm nevertheless. She couldn't talk anymore about death, about loneliness and things ending. It wasn't as if she were leaving him.

One night when they were still in the same warm bed together, she had had to turn her back to him, leave the bed finally, and she doesn't want that to happen again. Now she goes to him when she is sure there is no black mood, and they have good chats while she rubs his back.

She has, by piecing the stakes back together, one at a time, found their plots. "Here we are," she says. And he's off again, raging back to the car, stumbling in and out among gravestones, walking *over* some of the graves. He doesn't know how he hurts her, he can't know.

When she gets back to the car, she sees he is sitting behind the steering wheel, his hands white with the force of his grip. She gets in, does up her seat belt, and tucks her notebook into her purse. She is weak with anger.

She dreams him in their bed, and she is at the bedroom mirror. Turn around, he says, turn around. But she is looking at her own face, examining the lines and shadows and hollows. Bring your face to me, he calls, I can tell you what it means. She doesn't turn.

And now they have to die. She can see two of the kids standing motionless over a grave. Their thoughts leak out through their eyes, and she is proud of their thoughts. The other three are sobbing, their breathing irregular, their thoughts without order.

If it is to be him standing with them over her grave, he will want their support. Those shoulders will heave, and he won't stand straight. And she will be floating somewhere above them, wishing she could hold the grieving ones, knowing the others can make their own comfort.

But if it is to be her standing with them over his grave, she will sense him in the air around her, holding her. She will hear his joy or his rage and she will miss him, oh, she will miss him.

She turns to him, the one she will miss, and she sees on his outrageous face the beginning of a grin. She cannot, though she tries with all the might she can muster, contain herself. She is roaring with it, her head thrown back, her hands on her stomach, her teary eyes on his.

McCourt Fiction Series

In the spring of 1983, Coteau Books announced its
McCourt Fiction Series, a new venture in high-quality
fiction by prairie writers. The series is named in honour
of Edward A. McCourt (1907-1972), the distinguished
Canadian writer, critic, and teacher.

Ed McCourt's thirteen books of fiction, non-fiction, and
criticism are a vital part of the literary culture of
Saskatchewan and Canada. They include six fine novels,
non-fiction books on Saskatchewan, Canada, and the
Yukon and Northwest Territories, a biography, *Remember
Butler,* and a pioneering critical work, *The Canadian West
in Fiction.*

McCourt's influence as a vibrant and dedicated teacher
at the University of Saskatchewan has been no less
important. He won the respect and love of his students,
many of whom became teachers or writers themselves.
Wherever they are found, throughout Saskatchewan and
Canada, they remember the intellectual excitement of
their classes with Ed McCourt.

COTEAU BOOKS is pleased to release the fifth book
in the *McCourt Fiction Series* —
Women of Influence
by Bonnie Burnard.

Fiction from Coteau Books

Other fiction from Coteau Books is listed below. You may purchase or order any of these titles from your favorite bookstore. For a complete catalogue of publications—fiction, poetry, drama, criticism, non-fiction and children's literature—please write to 401 – 2206 Dewdney Avenue, Regina, Saskatchewan S4R 1H3.

The McCourt Fiction Series

Women of Influence by Bonnie Burnard. McCourt Fiction Series 5. Named Best First Book in the Commonwealth Writers Prize, 1989. In its third printing. $10.95(pbk)

The Wednesday Flower Man by Dianne Warren. McCourt Fiction Series 4. Witty and whimsical fiction. $10.95(pbk)

Night Games by Robert Currie. McCourt Fiction Series 1. Poignant stories about adolescence in the fifties. $7.00(pbk)

More Fiction from Coteau Books

100% Cracked Wheat edited by Robert Currie, Gary Hyland and Jim McLean. A side-splitting collection of stories and verse. In its third printing. $6.95 (pbk)

Best Kept Secrets by Pat Krause. Award-winning stories from a Regina writer. $21.95(cl), $10.95(pbk)

Duets by Per Brask and George Szanto. Sixteen short stories, the product of a unique collaboration. $10.95(pbk)

Foreigners by Barbara Sapergia. A sensitive portrayal of a Romanian immigrant family on the Prairies at the turn of the century. In its second printing. $6.95(pbk)

The Last India Overland by Craig Grant. An enthralling novel set in 1978. $7.95(pbk)

More Saskatchewan Gold edited by Geoffrey Ursell. Imaginative and masterful short stories from Saskatchewan writers. $6.95(pbk)

The Old Dance: Love Stories of One Sort or Another edited by Bonnie Burnard. Thirty short stories that examine love. $6.95(pbk)

Out of Place: Stories and Poems edited by Ven Begamudré and Judith Krause. Work by 37 authors on cultural displacement. $14.95(pbk)

Queen of the Headaches by Sharon Butala. This collection was nominated for the Governor-General's fiction award in 1985. In its third printing. $6.95(pbk)

Sky High: Stories from Saskatchewan edited by Geoffrey Ursell. Twenty-four stories from Saskatchewan writers. $6.95(pbk)

The Valley of Flowers: A Story of a TB Sanatorium by Veronica Eddy Brock. A popular novel about the experiences of a young girl confined to a TB sanatorium during the forties. In its second printing. $6.95(pbk)

Wishbone by Reg Silvester. Seven short stories and a novella about the Condon family, a member of which possesses a magical rib, a wishbone. $21.95 (cl), $9.95(pbk)

Working without a Laugh Track by Fred Stenson. A collection of twelve funny, often outrageous short stories. An update of the age-old battle of the sexes from a male point of view. $21.95 (cl), $10.95(pbk)

Bonnie Burnard

*Bonnie Burnard's stories have appeared in numerous
literary journals and anthologies:* Canadian Short Stories
(Oxford, 1991); SoHo Square III *(Bloomsbury Press, 1990);*
Sky High *(Coteau, 1988);* More Saskatchewan Gold
(Coteau, 1984); Best Canadian Stories '84 *(Oberon, 1984);*
Coming Attractions *(Oberon, 1983); and* Saskatchewan
Gold *(Coteau, 1982); Since* Women of Influence *won Best
First Book of the Commonwealth Writers Prize in 1989,
Burnard has read and lectured in Australia, Great Britain,
the United States, Sweden, Germany and across Canada.
Stories from* Women of Influence *have been adapted for
television and radio.*

About the Artist

Elyse St. George, the artist featured on the cover of
Women of Influence, *is a painter and writer living in
Saskatoon. Her book,* White Lions in the afternoon, *a
collection of poetry and etchings, was published by Coteau
Books in 1987.*